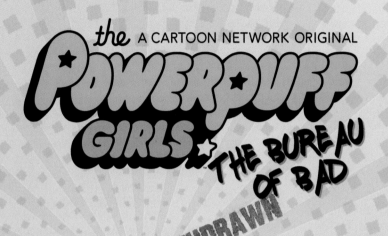

A CARTOON NETWORK ORIGINAL

the POWERPUFF GIRLS

THE BUREAU OF BAD

WITHDRAWN

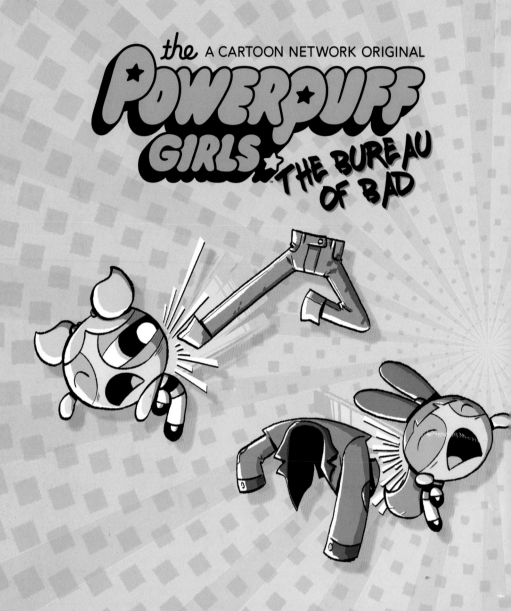

the A CARTOON NETWORK ORIGINAL

POWERPUFF GIRLS™ THE BUREAU OF BAD

Special thanks to Marisa Marionakis and Janet No of Cartoon Network.

For international rights, contact **licensing@idwpublishing.com**

978-1-68405-247-9

21 20 19 18 1 2 3 4

IDW® CN CARTOON NETWORK.

www.IDWPUBLISHING.com

Greg Goldstein, President & Publisher • **Robbie Robbins**, EVP/Sr. Art Director • **Chris Ryall,** Chief Creative Officer & Editor-in-Chief
Matthew Ruzicka, CPA, Chief Financial Officer • **David Hedgecock**, Associate Publisher • **Laurie Windrow**, Senior Vice President of Sales & Marketing • **Lorelei Bunjes**, VP of Digital Services • **Eric Moss**, Sr. Director, Licensing & Business Development

Ted Adams, Founder & CEO of IDW Media Holdings

Facebook: **facebook.com/idwpublishing** • Twitter: **@idwpublishing** • YouTube: **youtube.com/idwpublishing**
Tumblr: **tumblr.idwpublishing.com** • Instagram: **instagram.com/idwpublishing**

Originally published as THE POWERPUFF GIRLS: BUREAU OF BAD issues #1–3.

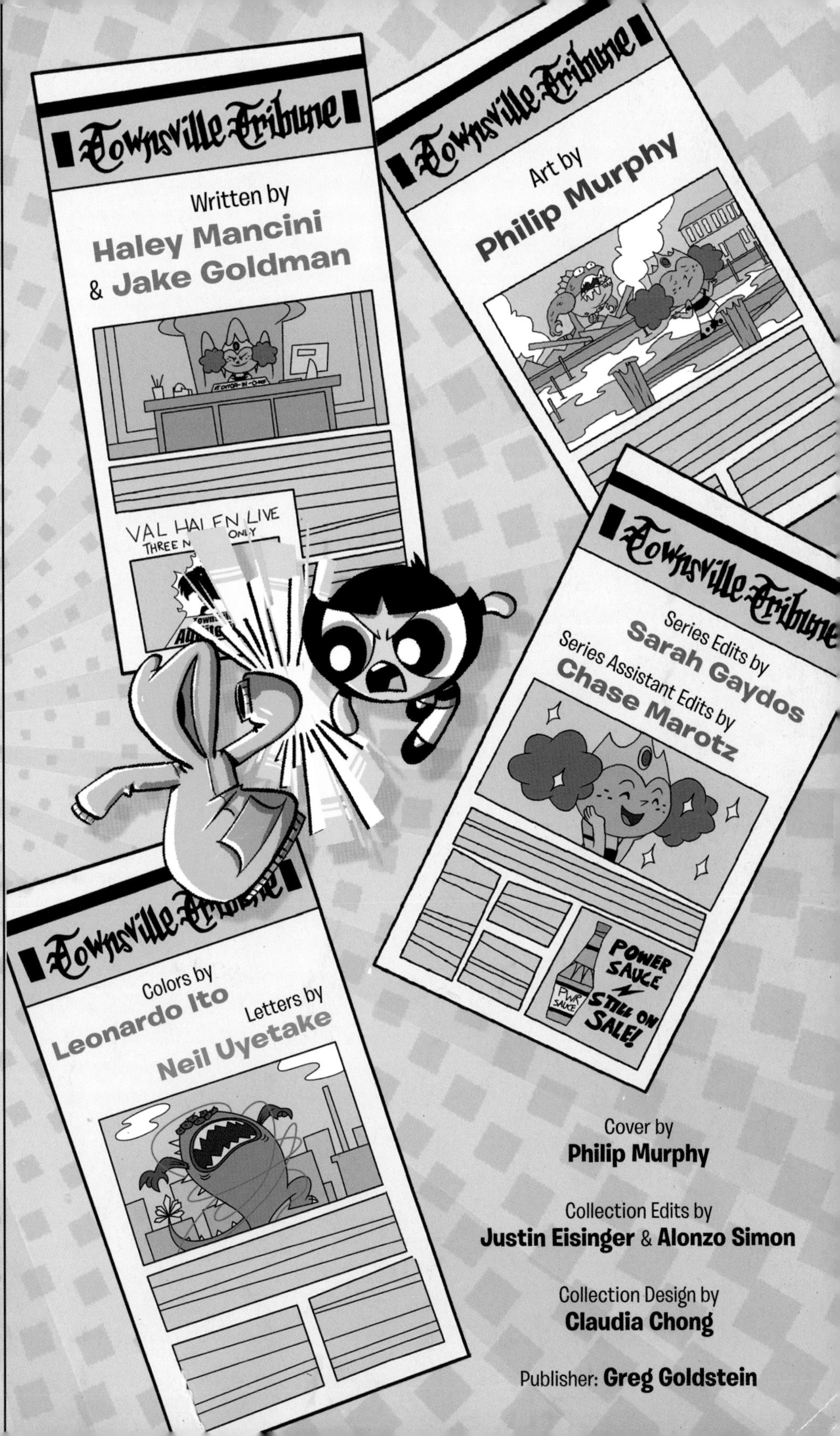
Townsville Tribune
Written by
Haley Mancini
& Jake Goldman
EDITOR-IN-CHIEF
VAL HALEN LIVE
Townsville Tribune
Art by
Philip Murphy
Townsville Tribune
Series Edits by
Sarah Gaydos
Series Assistant Edits by
Chase Marotz
POWER SAUCE
STILL ON SALE!
PWR SAUCE
Townsville Tribune
Colors by
Leonardo Ito
Letters by
Neil Uyetake

Cover by
Philip Murphy

Collection Edits by
Justin Eisinger & **Alonzo Simon**

Collection Design by
Claudia Chong

Publisher: **Greg Goldstein**

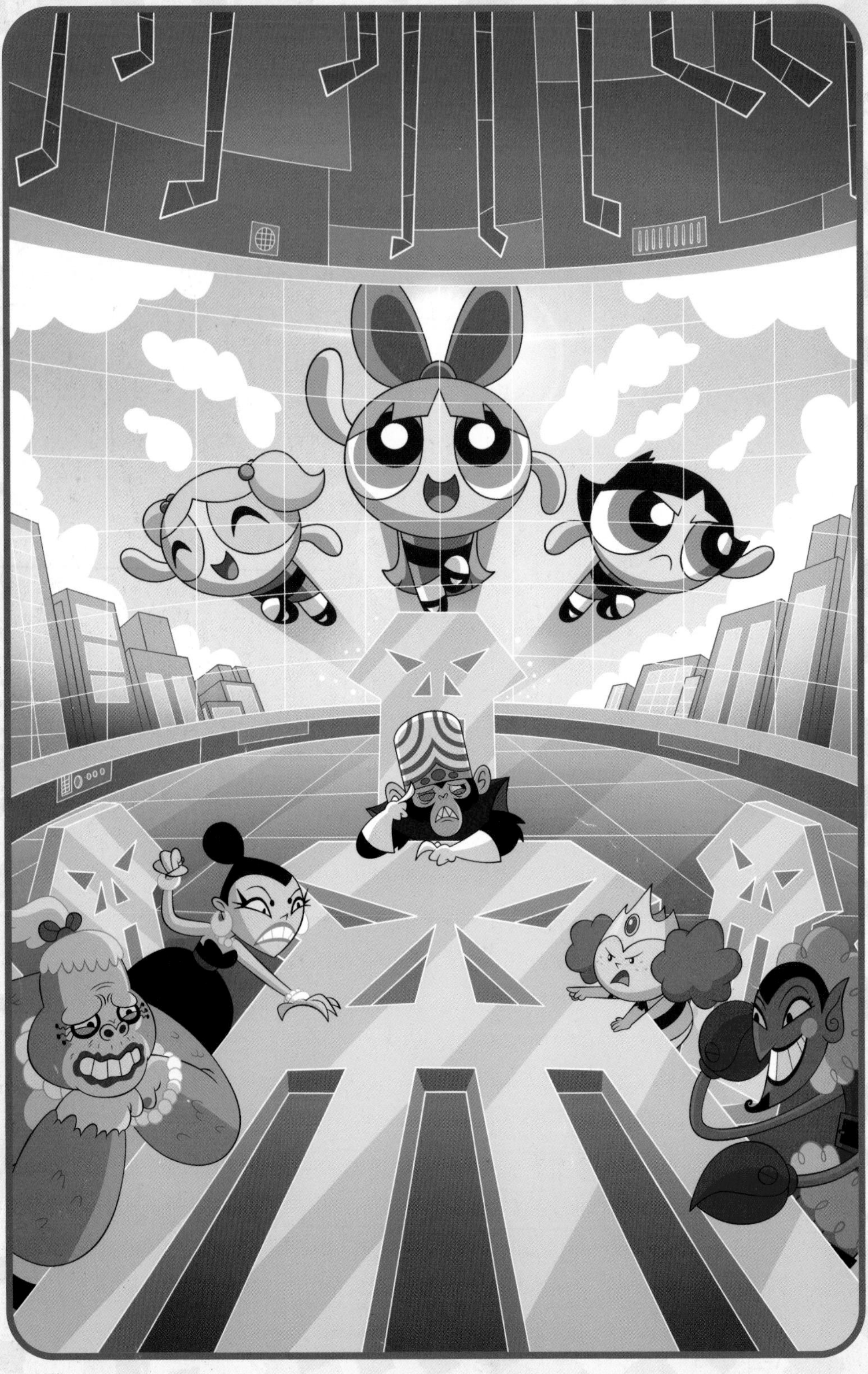

Cover Art by **Philip Murphy**

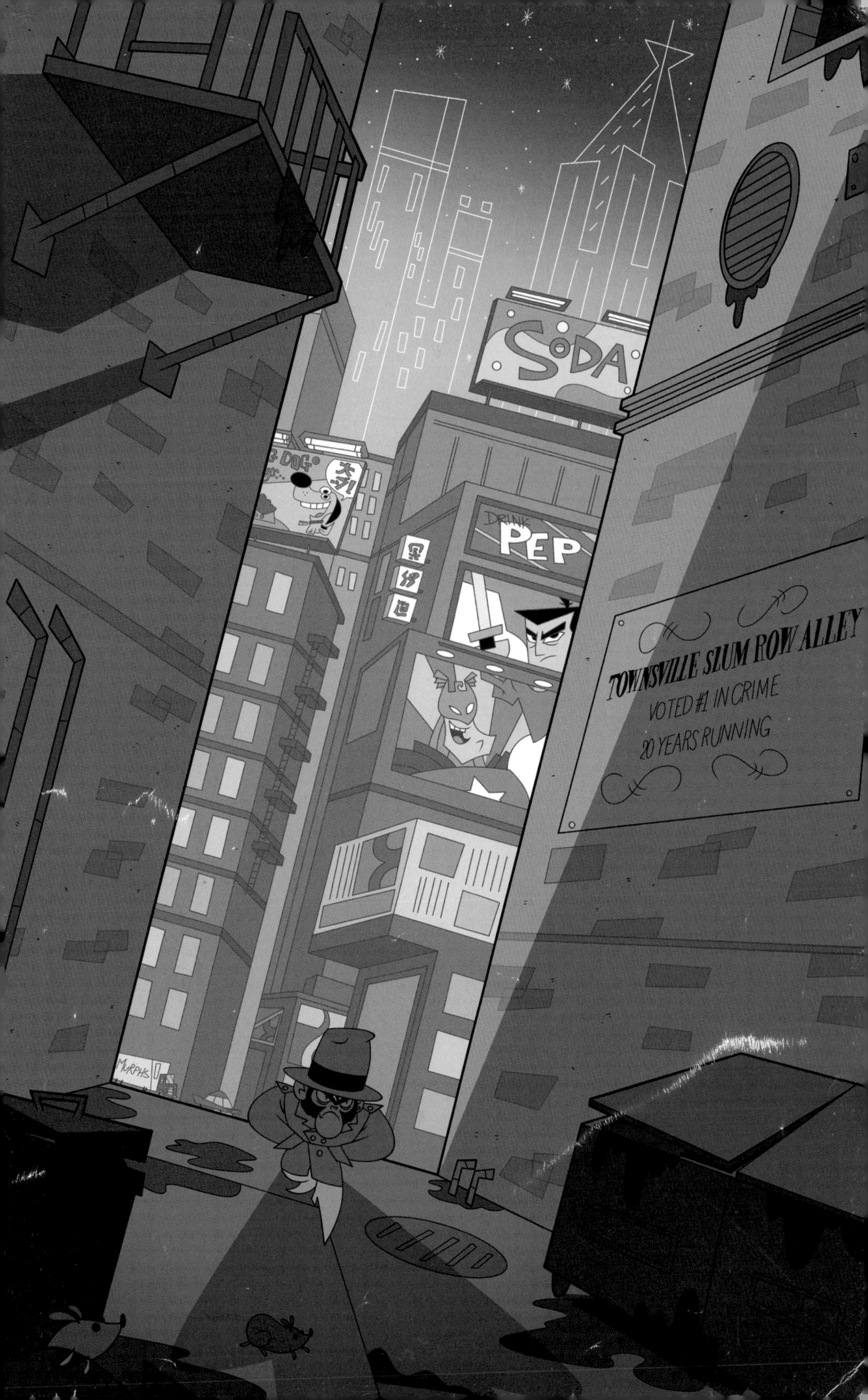
SODA
DRINK
PEP
TOWNSVILLE SLUM ROW ALLEY
VOTED #1 IN CRIME
20 YEARS RUNNING
MURPHS

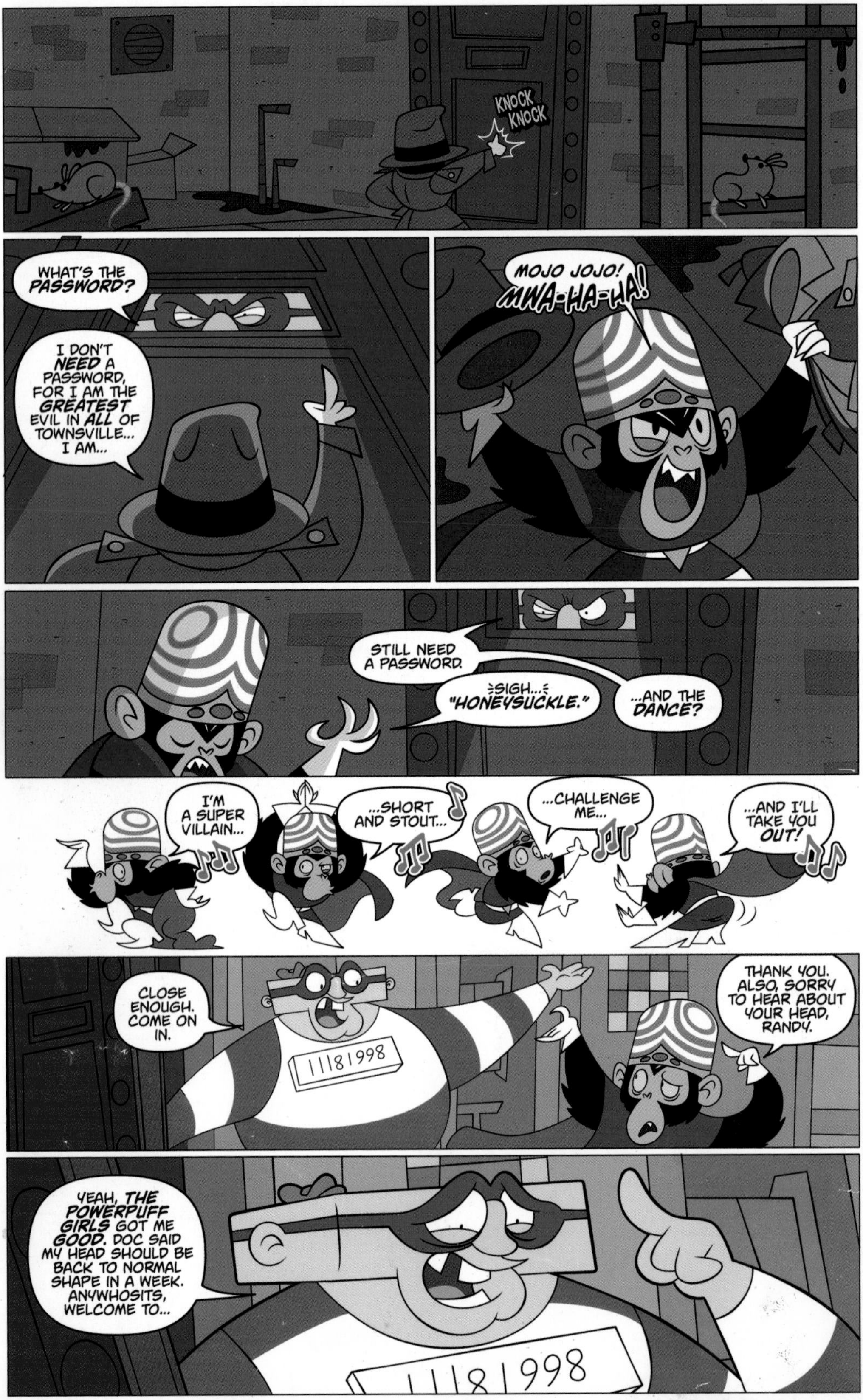
KNOCK KNOCK
WHAT'S THE PASSWORD?
I DON'T NEED A PASSWORD, FOR I AM THE GREATEST EVIL IN ALL OF TOWNSVILLE... I AM...
MOJO JOJO! MWA-HA-HA!
STILL NEED A PASSWORD.
SIGH... "HONEYSUCKLE."
...AND THE DANCE?
I'M A SUPER VILLAIN...
...SHORT AND STOUT...
...CHALLENGE ME...
...AND I'LL TAKE YOU OUT!
CLOSE ENOUGH. COME ON IN.
11181998
THANK YOU. ALSO, SORRY TO HEAR ABOUT YOUR HEAD, RANDY.
YEAH, THE POWERPUFF GIRLS GOT ME GOOD. DOC SAID MY HEAD SHOULD BE BACK TO NORMAL SHAPE IN A WEEK. ANYWHOSITS, WELCOME TO...
11181998

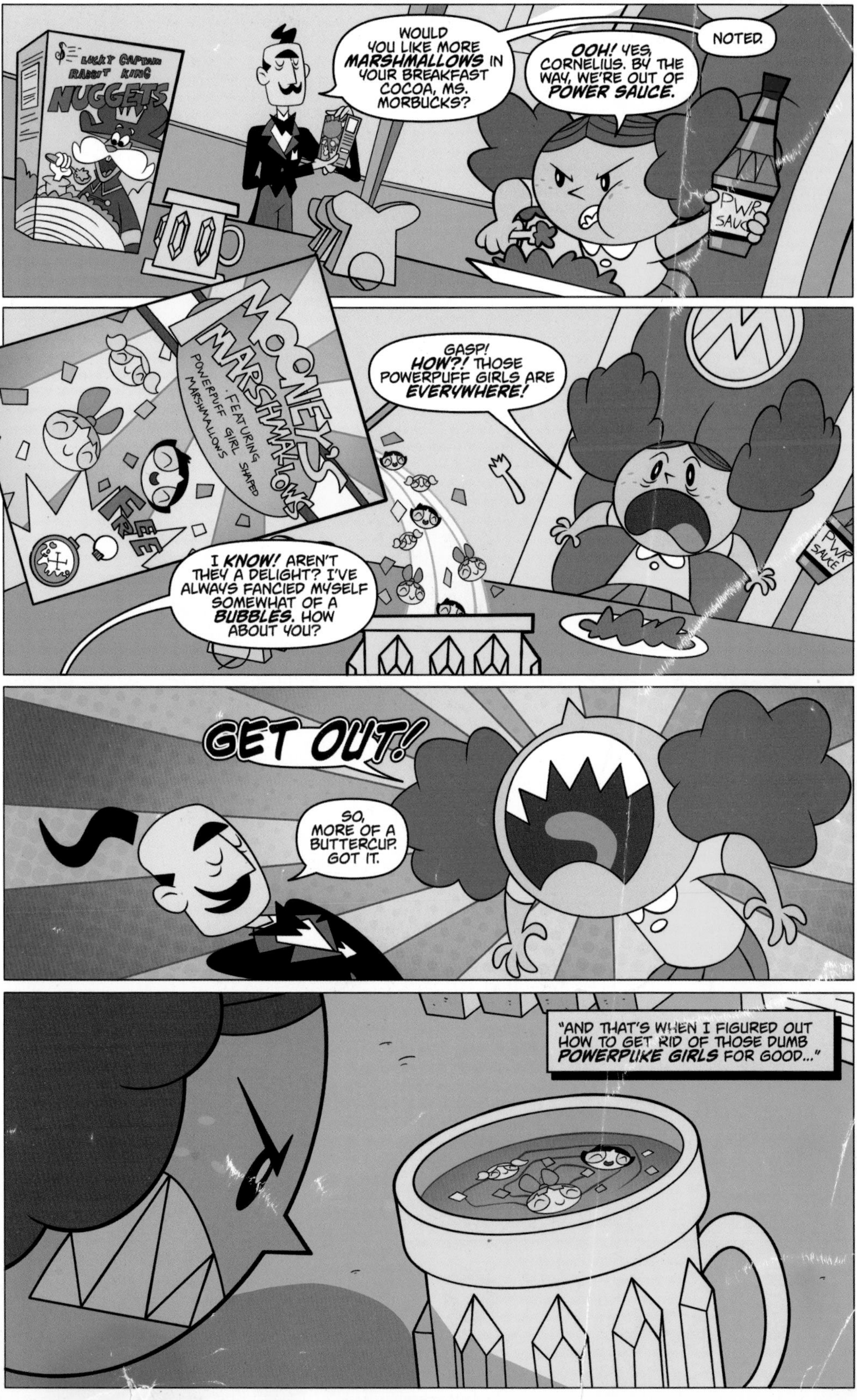
LUCKY CAPTAIN RABBIT KING NUGGETS
WOULD YOU LIKE MORE MARSHMALLOWS IN YOUR BREAKFAST COCOA, MS. MORBUCKS?
OOH! YES, CORNELIUS. BY THE WAY, WE'RE OUT OF POWER SAUCE.
NOTED.
PWR SAUCE
MOONEY'S MARSHMALLOWS
FEATURING POWERPUFF GIRL SHAPED MARSHMALLOWS
FREE
GASP! HOW?! THOSE POWERPUFF GIRLS ARE EVERYWHERE!
I KNOW! AREN'T THEY A DELIGHT? I'VE ALWAYS FANCIED MYSELF SOMEWHAT OF A BUBBLES. HOW ABOUT YOU?
PWR SAUCE
GET OUT!
SO, MORE OF A BUTTERCUP. GOT IT.
"AND THAT'S WHEN I FIGURED OUT HOW TO GET RID OF THOSE DUMB POWERPUKE GIRLS FOR GOOD..."

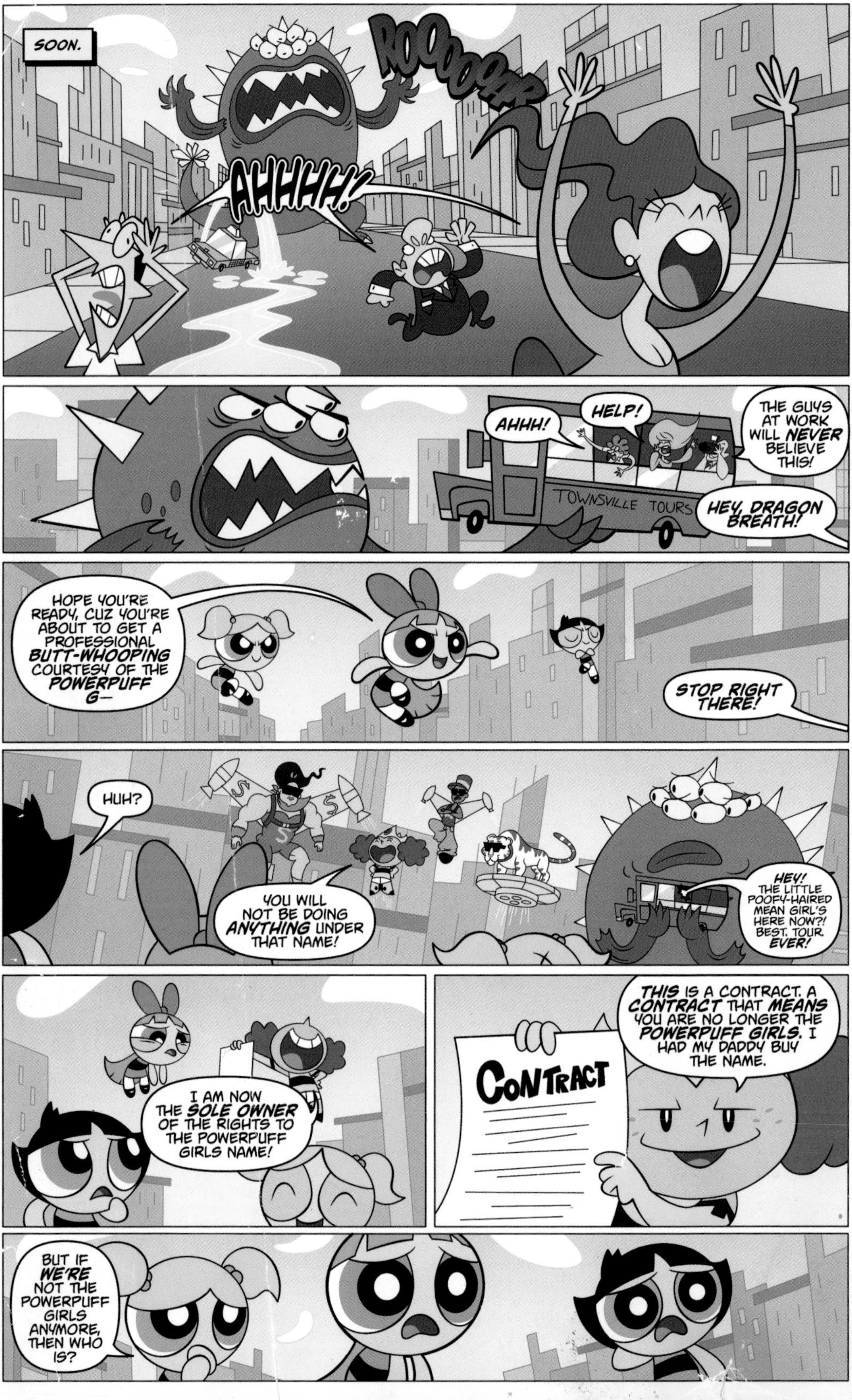
SOON.
ROOOOOAR
AHHHH!
AHHH!
HELP!
THE GUYS AT WORK WILL NEVER BELIEVE THIS!
TOWNSVILLE TOURS
HEY, DRAGON BREATH!
HOPE YOU'RE READY, CUZ YOU'RE ABOUT TO GET A PROFESSIONAL BUTT-WHOOPING COURTESY OF THE POWERPUFF G—
STOP RIGHT THERE!
HUH?
YOU WILL NOT BE DOING ANYTHING UNDER THAT NAME!
HEY! THE LITTLE POOFY-HAIRED MEAN GIRL'S HERE NOW?! BEST. TOUR. EVER!
I AM NOW THE SOLE OWNER OF THE RIGHTS TO THE POWERPUFF GIRLS NAME!
THIS IS A CONTRACT. A CONTRACT THAT MEANS YOU ARE NO LONGER THE POWERPUFF GIRLS. I HAD MY DADDY BUY THE NAME.
CONTRACT
BUT IF WE'RE NOT THE POWERPUFF GIRLS ANYMORE, THEN WHO IS?

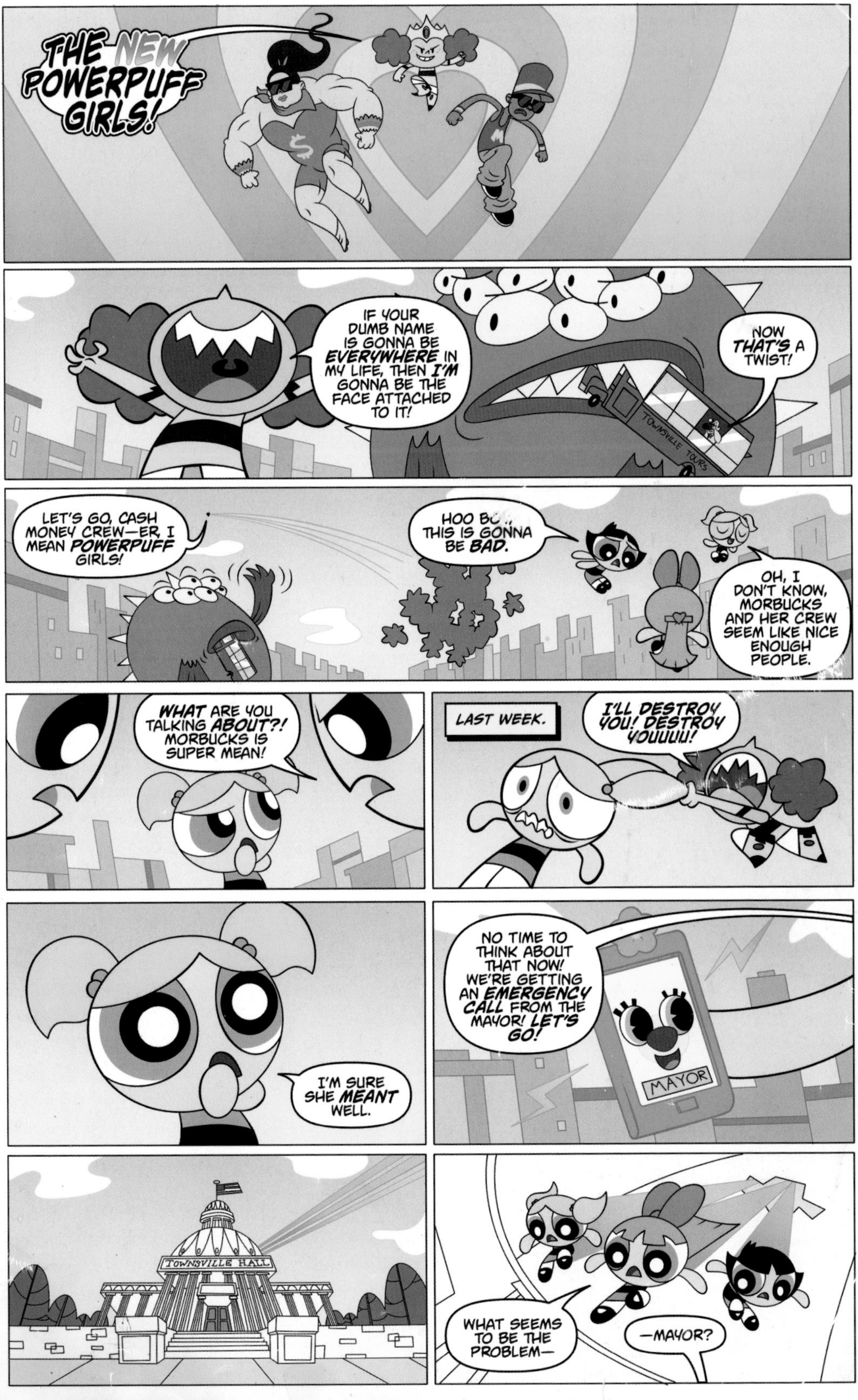
THE NEW POWERPUFF GIRLS!
IF YOUR DUMB NAME IS GONNA BE EVERYWHERE IN MY LIFE, THEN I'M GONNA BE THE FACE ATTACHED TO IT!
TOWNSVILLE TOURS
NOW THAT'S A TWIST!
LET'S GO, CASH MONEY CREW—ER, I MEAN POWERPUFF GIRLS!
HOO BO THIS IS GONNA BE BAD.
OH, I DON'T KNOW, MORBUCKS AND HER CREW SEEM LIKE NICE ENOUGH PEOPLE.
WHAT ARE YOU TALKING ABOUT?! MORBUCKS IS SUPER MEAN!
LAST WEEK.
I'LL DESTROY YOU! DESTROY YOUUUU!
I'M SURE SHE MEANT WELL.
NO TIME TO THINK ABOUT THAT NOW! WE'RE GETTING AN EMERGENCY CALL FROM THE MAYOR! LET'S GO!
MAYOR
TOWNSVILLE HALL
WHAT SEEMS TO BE THE PROBLEM—
—MAYOR?

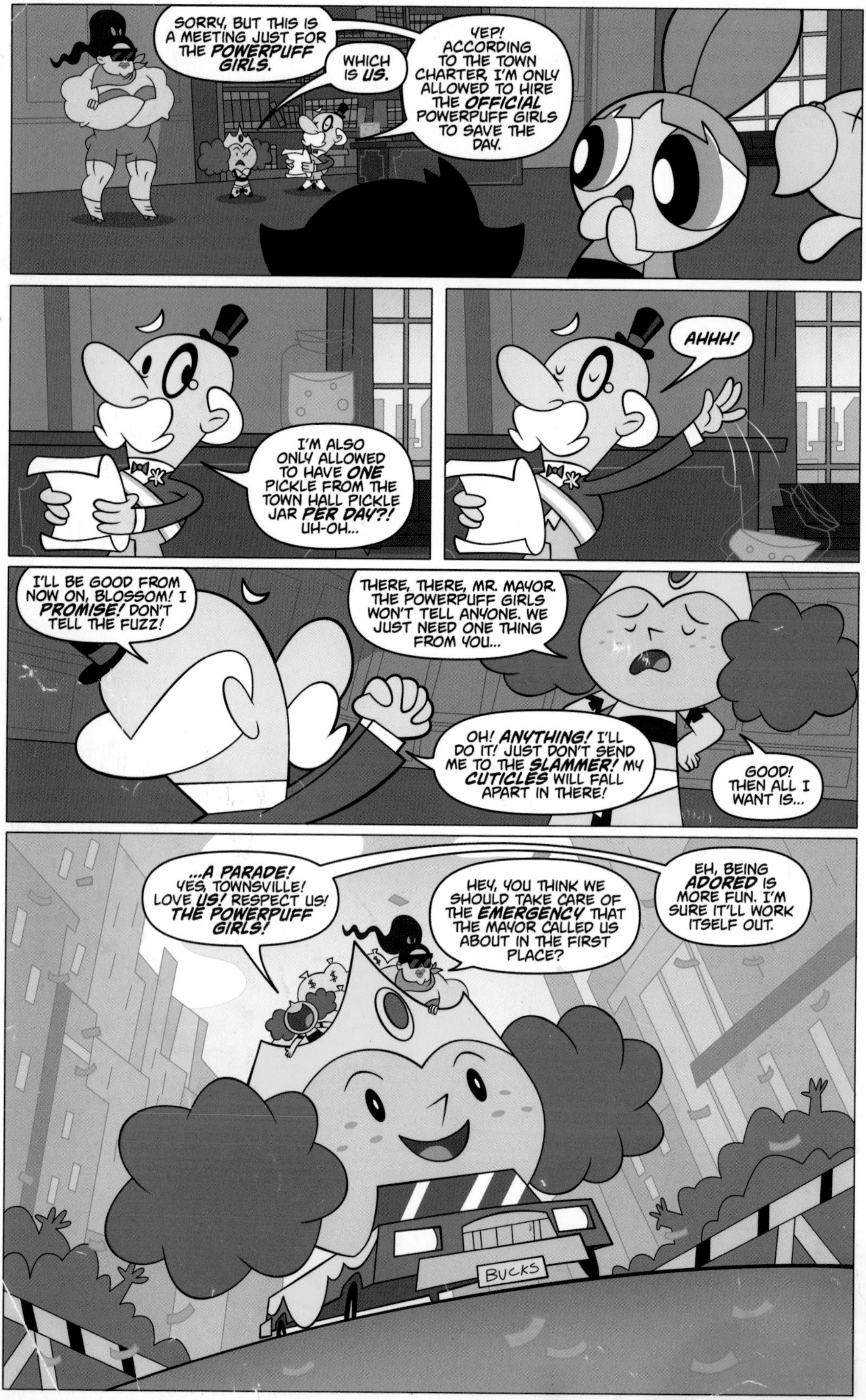
SORRY, BUT THIS IS A MEETING JUST FOR THE POWERPUFF GIRLS.
WHICH IS US.
YEP! ACCORDING TO THE TOWN CHARTER, I'M ONLY ALLOWED TO HIRE THE OFFICIAL POWERPUFF GIRLS TO SAVE THE DAY.
I'M ALSO ONLY ALLOWED TO HAVE ONE PICKLE FROM THE TOWN HALL PICKLE JAR PER DAY?! UH-OH...
AHHH!
I'LL BE GOOD FROM NOW ON, BLOSSOM! I PROMISE! DON'T TELL THE FUZZ!
THERE, THERE, MR. MAYOR. THE POWERPUFF GIRLS WON'T TELL ANYONE. WE JUST NEED ONE THING FROM YOU...
OH! ANYTHING! I'LL DO IT! JUST DON'T SEND ME TO THE SLAMMER! MY CUTICLES WILL FALL APART IN THERE!
GOOD! THEN ALL I WANT IS...
...A PARADE! YES, TOWNSVILLE! LOVE US! RESPECT US! THE POWERPUFF GIRLS!
HEY, YOU THINK WE SHOULD TAKE CARE OF THE EMERGENCY THAT THE MAYOR CALLED US ABOUT IN THE FIRST PLACE?
EH, BEING ADORED IS MORE FUN. I'M SURE IT'LL WORK ITSELF OUT.
BUCKS

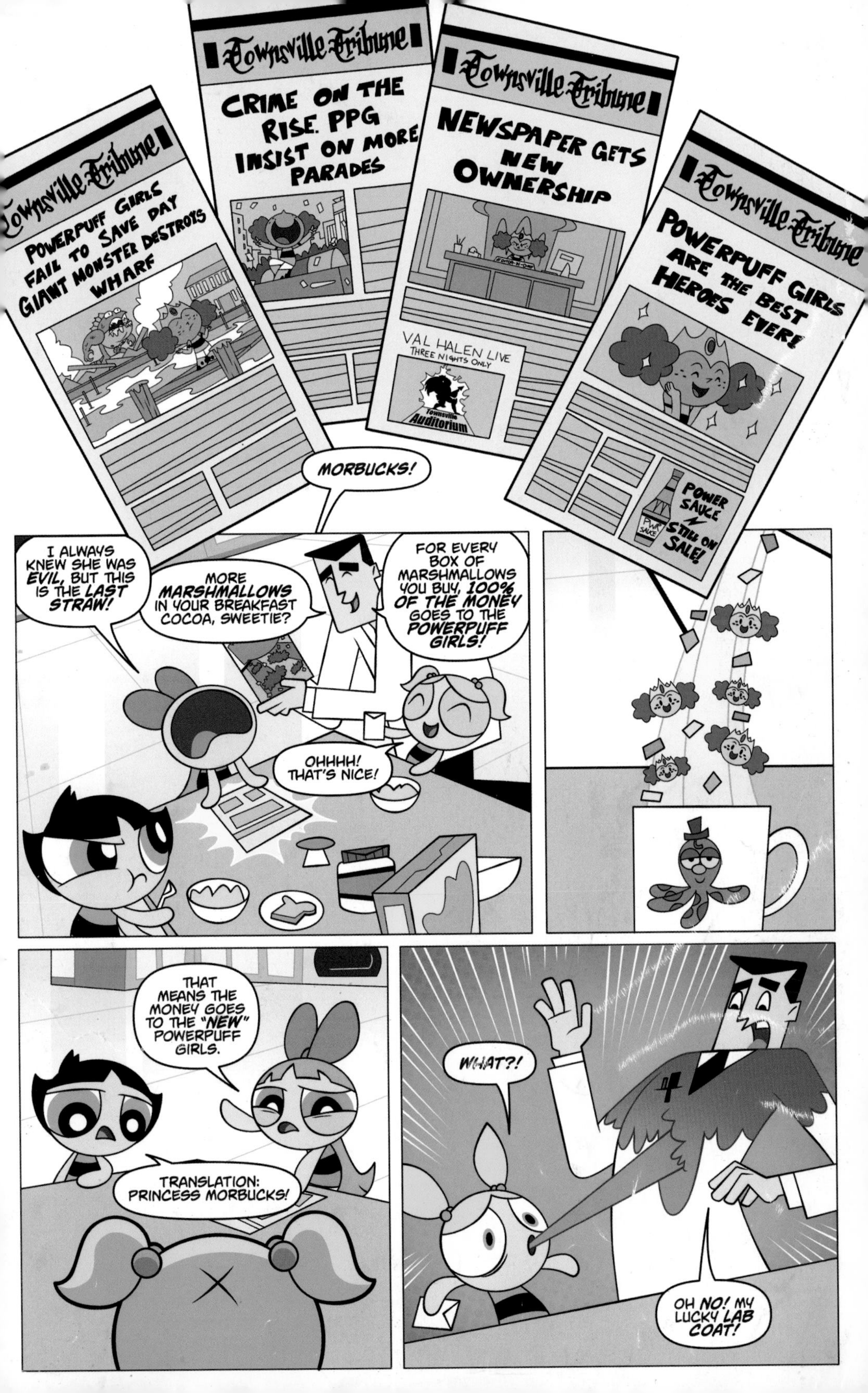
Townsville Tribune
POWERPUFF GIRLS FAIL TO SAVE DAY GIANT MONSTER DESTROYS WHARF
Townsville Tribune
CRIME ON THE RISE. PPG INSIST ON MORE PARADES
Townsville Tribune
NEWSPAPER GETS NEW OWNERSHIP
VAL HALEN LIVE
THREE NIGHTS ONLY
Townsville Auditorium
Townsville Tribune
POWERPUFF GIRLS ARE THE BEST HEROES EVER!
POWER SAUCE STILL ON SALE!
PWR SAUCE
MORBUCKS!
I ALWAYS KNEW SHE WAS EVIL, BUT THIS IS THE LAST STRAW!
MORE MARSHMALLOWS IN YOUR BREAKFAST COCOA, SWEETIE?
FOR EVERY BOX OF MARSHMALLOWS YOU BUY, 100% OF THE MONEY GOES TO THE POWERPUFF GIRLS!
OHHHH! THAT'S NICE!
THAT MEANS THE MONEY GOES TO THE "NEW" POWERPUFF GIRLS.
TRANSLATION: PRINCESS MORBUCKS!
WHAT?!
OH NO! MY LUCKY LAB COAT!

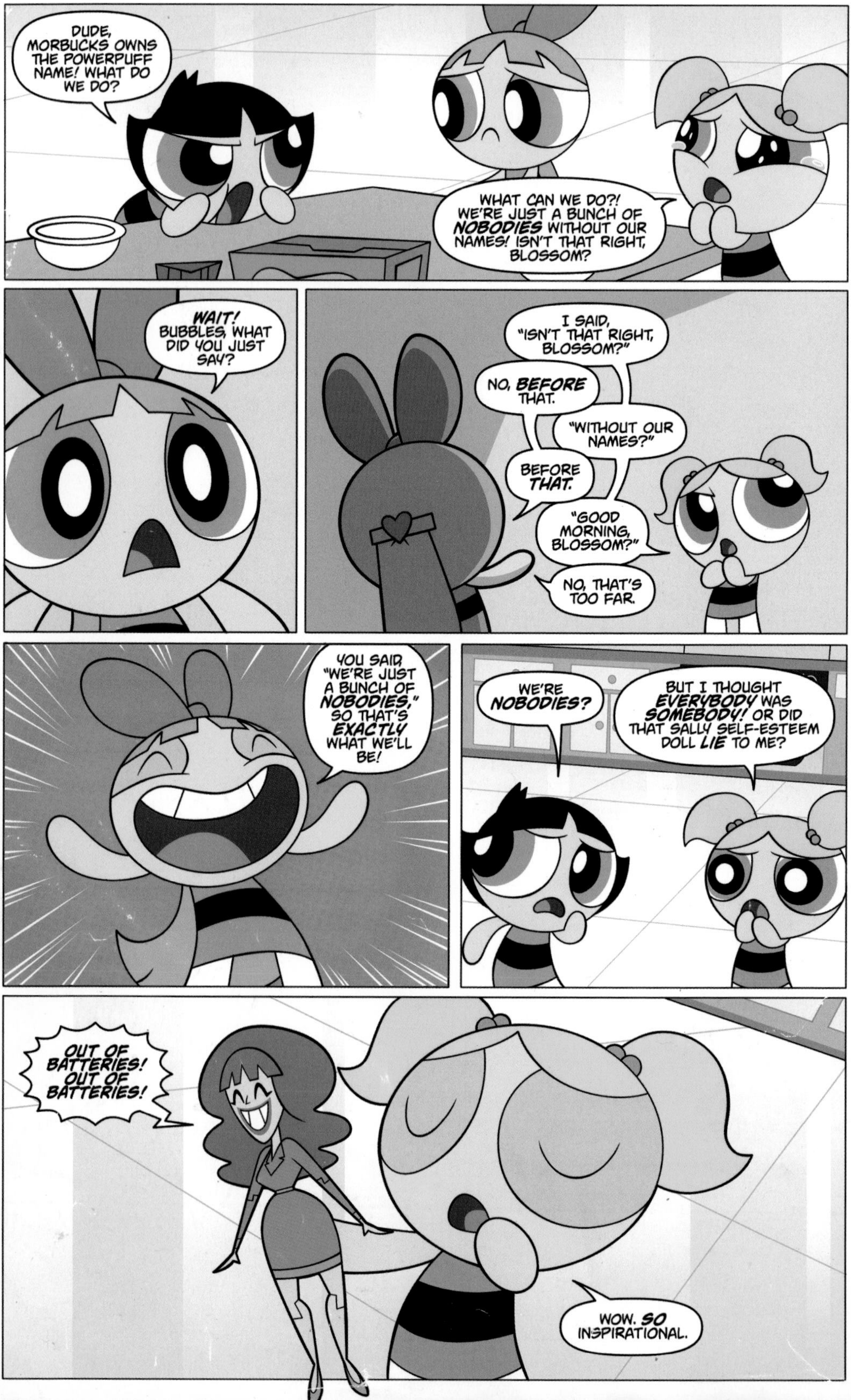
DUDE, MORBUCKS OWNS THE POWERPUFF NAME! WHAT DO WE DO?
WHAT CAN WE DO?! WE'RE JUST A BUNCH OF NOBODIES WITHOUT OUR NAMES! ISN'T THAT RIGHT, BLOSSOM?
WAIT! BUBBLES, WHAT DID YOU JUST SAY?
I SAID, "ISN'T THAT RIGHT, BLOSSOM?"
NO, BEFORE THAT.
"WITHOUT OUR NAMES?"
BEFORE THAT.
"GOOD MORNING, BLOSSOM?"
NO, THAT'S TOO FAR.
YOU SAID, "WE'RE JUST A BUNCH OF NOBODIES," SO THAT'S EXACTLY WHAT WE'LL BE!
WE'RE NOBODIES?
BUT I THOUGHT EVERYBODY WAS SOMEBODY! OR DID THAT SALLY SELF-ESTEEM DOLL LIE TO ME?
OUT OF BATTERIES! OUT OF BATTERIES!
WOW. SO INSPIRATIONAL.

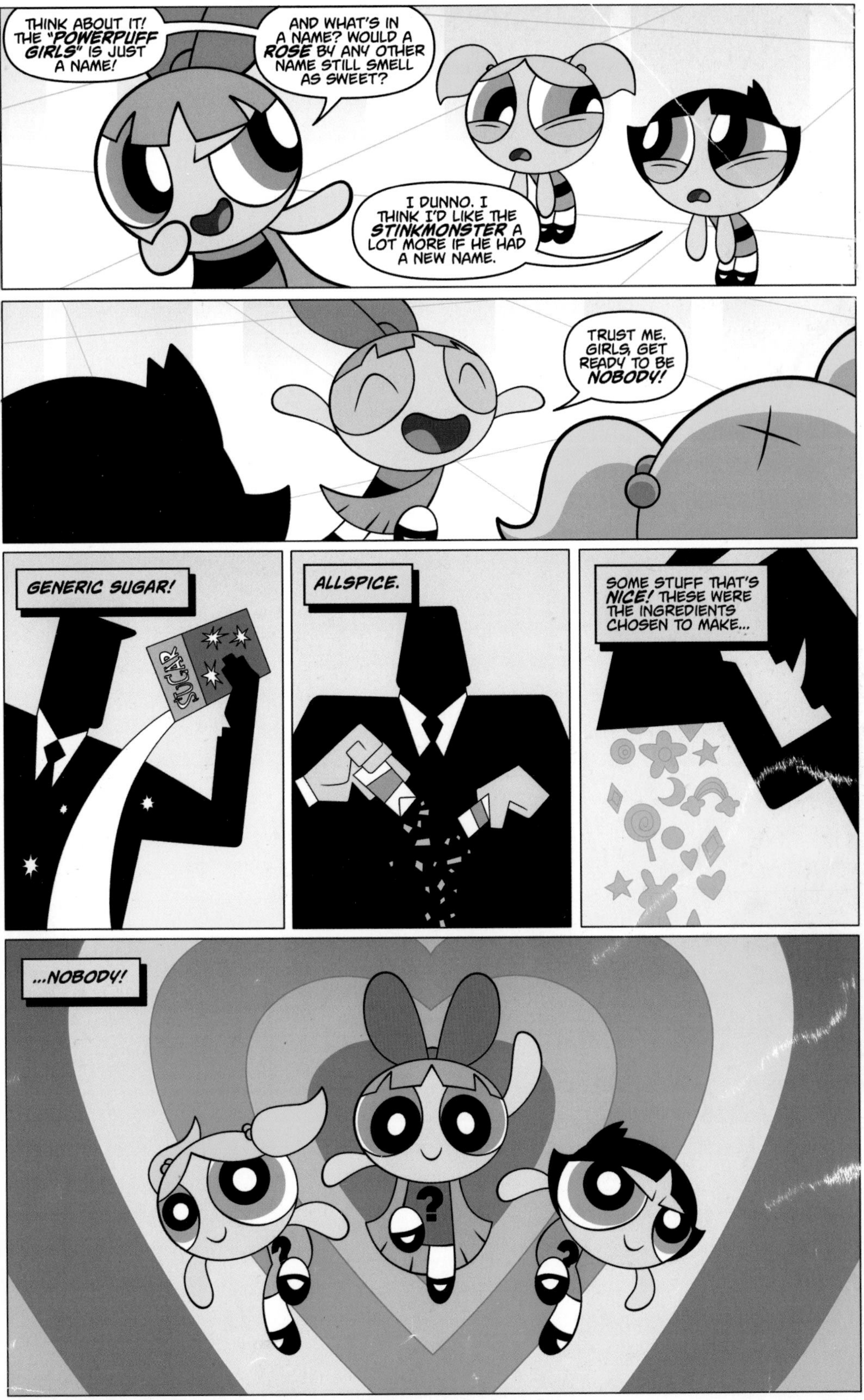

THINK ABOUT IT! THE "POWERPUFF GIRLS" IS JUST A NAME!
AND WHAT'S IN A NAME? WOULD A ROSE BY ANY OTHER NAME STILL SMELL AS SWEET?
I DUNNO. I THINK I'D LIKE THE STINKMONSTER A LOT MORE IF HE HAD A NEW NAME.
TRUST ME. GIRLS, GET READY TO BE NOBODY!
GENERIC SUGAR!
SUGAR
ALLSPICE.
SOME STUFF THAT'S NICE! THESE WERE THE INGREDIENTS CHOSEN TO MAKE...
...NOBODY!

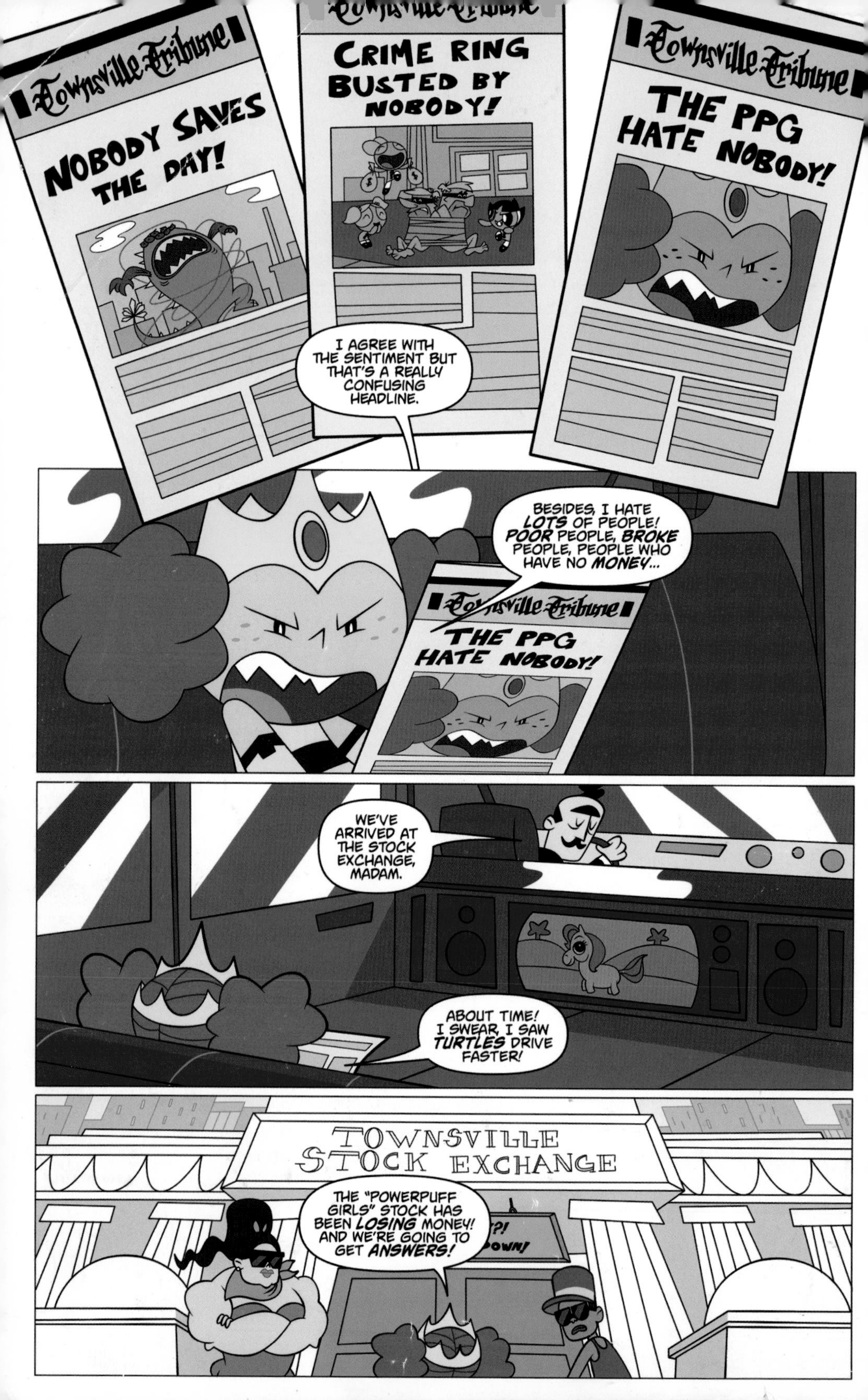

Townsville Tribune
NOBODY SAVES THE DAY!
CRIME RING BUSTED BY NOBODY!
Townsville Tribune
THE PPG HATE NOBODY!
I AGREE WITH THE SENTIMENT BUT THAT'S A REALLY CONFUSING HEADLINE.
BESIDES, I HATE LOTS OF PEOPLE! POOR PEOPLE, BROKE PEOPLE, PEOPLE WHO HAVE NO MONEY...
Townsville Tribune
THE PPG HATE NOBODY!
WE'VE ARRIVED AT THE STOCK EXCHANGE, MADAM.
ABOUT TIME! I SWEAR, I SAW TURTLES DRIVE FASTER!
TOWNSVILLE STOCK EXCHANGE
THE "POWERPUFF GIRLS" STOCK HAS BEEN LOSING MONEY! AND WE'RE GOING TO GET ANSWERS!

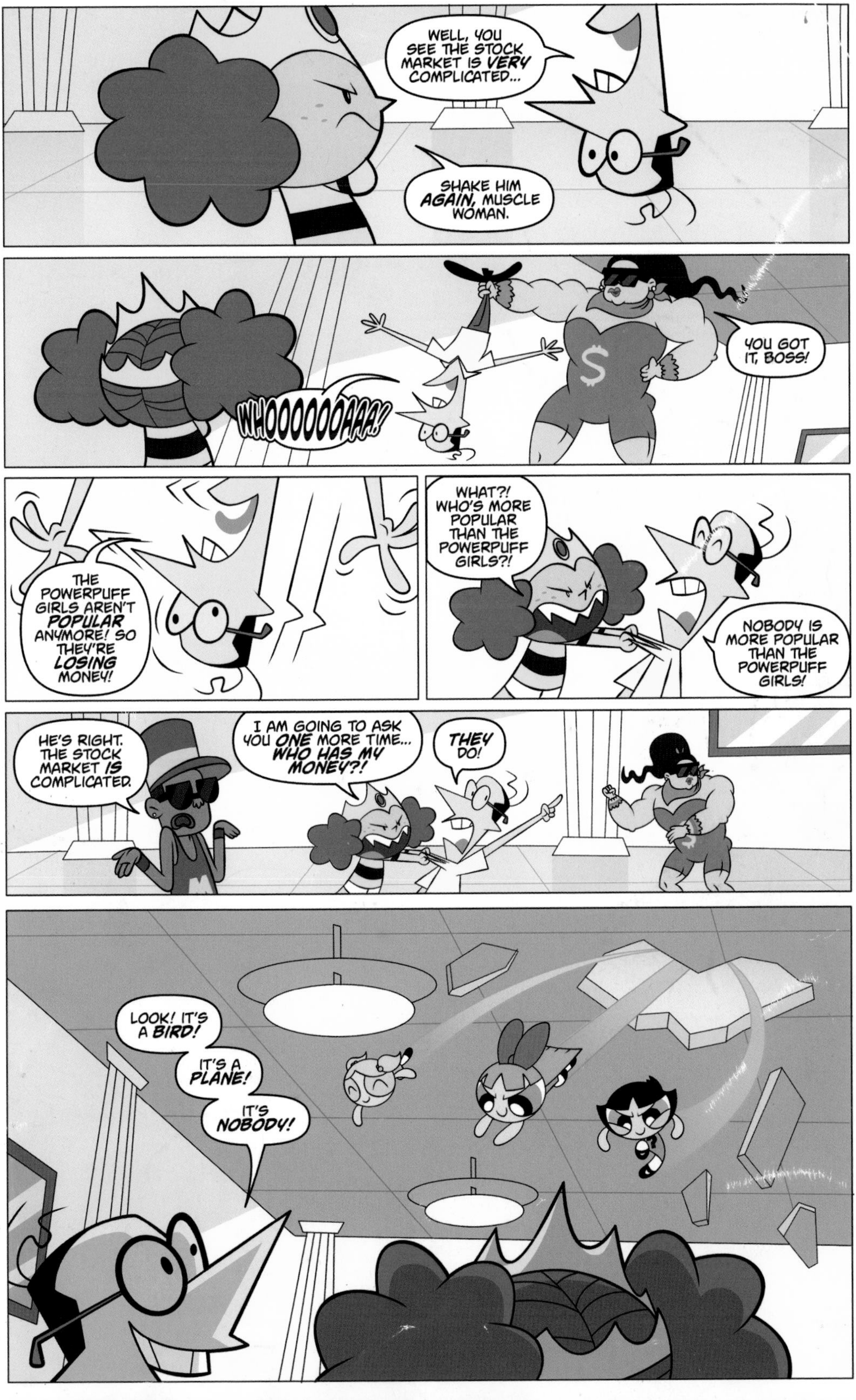

WELL, YOU SEE THE STOCK MARKET IS VERY COMPLICATED...
SHAKE HIM AGAIN, MUSCLE WOMAN.
YOU GOT IT, BOSS!
WHOOOOOOAAA!
THE POWERPUFF GIRLS AREN'T POPULAR ANYMORE! SO THEY'RE LOSING MONEY!
WHAT?! WHO'S MORE POPULAR THAN THE POWERPUFF GIRLS?!
NOBODY IS MORE POPULAR THAN THE POWERPUFF GIRLS!
HE'S RIGHT. THE STOCK MARKET IS COMPLICATED.
I AM GOING TO ASK YOU ONE MORE TIME... WHO HAS MY MONEY?!
THEY DO!
LOOK! IT'S A BIRD!
IT'S A PLANE!
IT'S NOBODY!

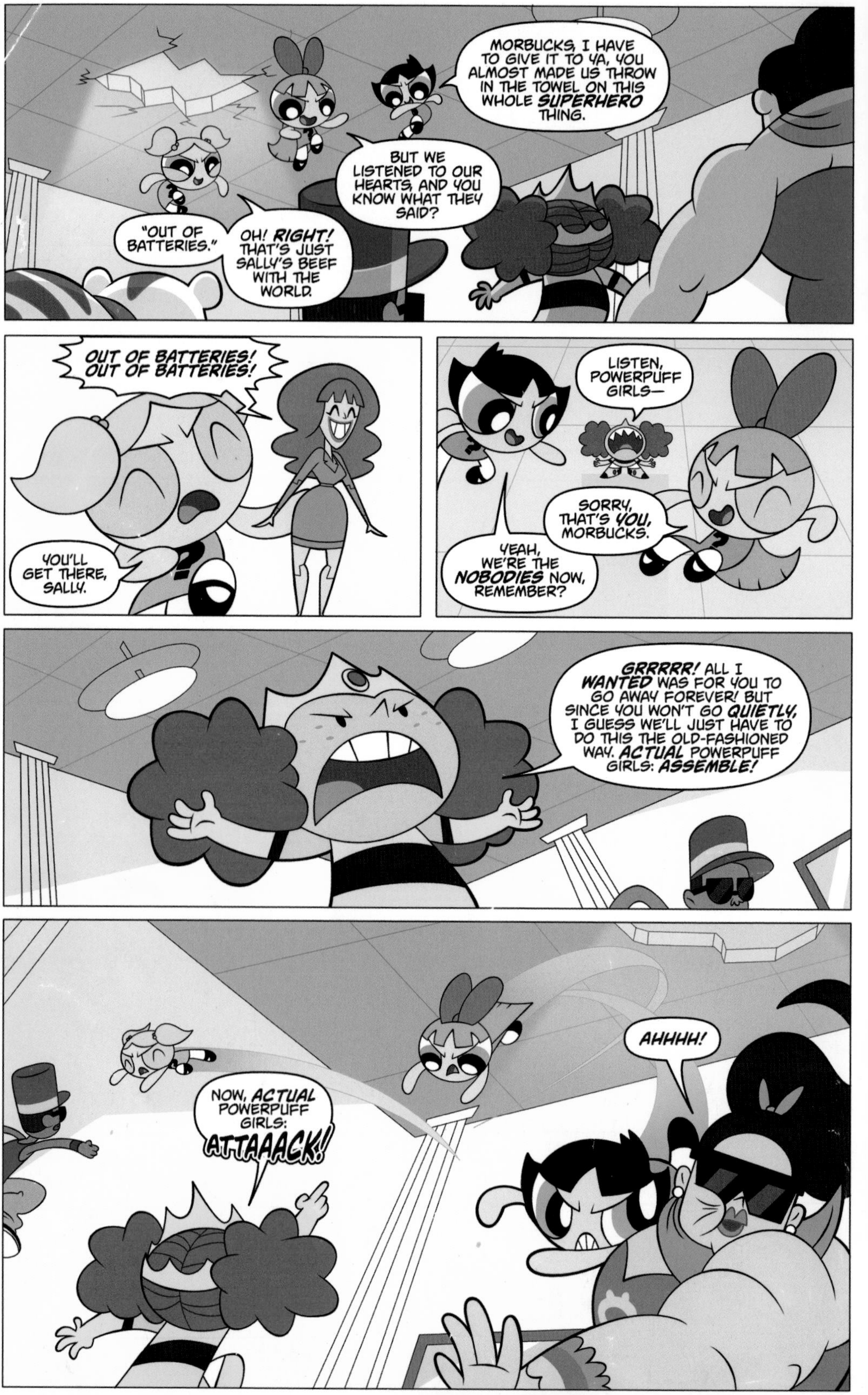
MORBUCKS, I HAVE TO GIVE IT TO YA, YOU ALMOST MADE US THROW IN THE TOWEL ON THIS WHOLE SUPERHERO THING.
BUT WE LISTENED TO OUR HEARTS, AND YOU KNOW WHAT THEY SAID?
"OUT OF BATTERIES."
OH! RIGHT! THAT'S JUST SALLY'S BEEF WITH THE WORLD.
OUT OF BATTERIES! OUT OF BATTERIES!
YOU'LL GET THERE, SALLY.
LISTEN, POWERPUFF GIRLS—
SORRY, THAT'S YOU, MORBUCKS.
YEAH, WE'RE THE NOBODIES NOW, REMEMBER?
GRRRRR! ALL I WANTED WAS FOR YOU TO GO AWAY FOREVER! BUT SINCE YOU WON'T GO QUIETLY, I GUESS WE'LL JUST HAVE TO DO THIS THE OLD-FASHIONED WAY. ACTUAL POWERPUFF GIRLS: ASSEMBLE!
NOW, ACTUAL POWERPUFF GIRLS: ATTAAACK!
AHHHH!

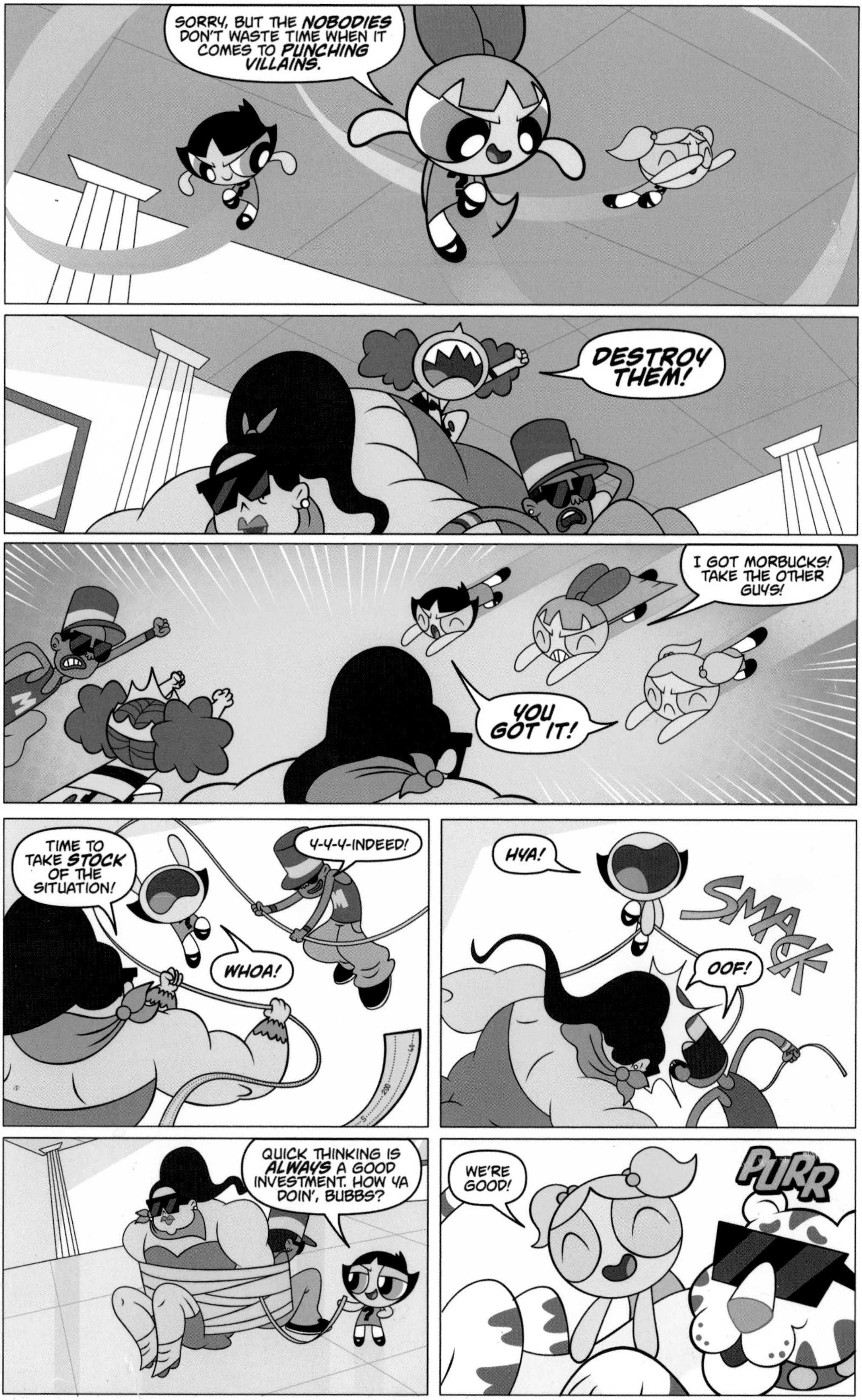
SORRY, BUT THE NOBODIES DON'T WASTE TIME WHEN IT COMES TO PUNCHING VILLAINS.
DESTROY THEM!
I GOT MORBUCKS! TAKE THE OTHER GUYS!
YOU GOT IT!
TIME TO TAKE STOCK OF THE SITUATION!
Y-Y-Y-INDEED!
WHOA!
HYA!
SMACK
OOF!
QUICK THINKING IS ALWAYS A GOOD INVESTMENT. HOW YA DOIN', BUBBS?
WE'RE GOOD!
PURR

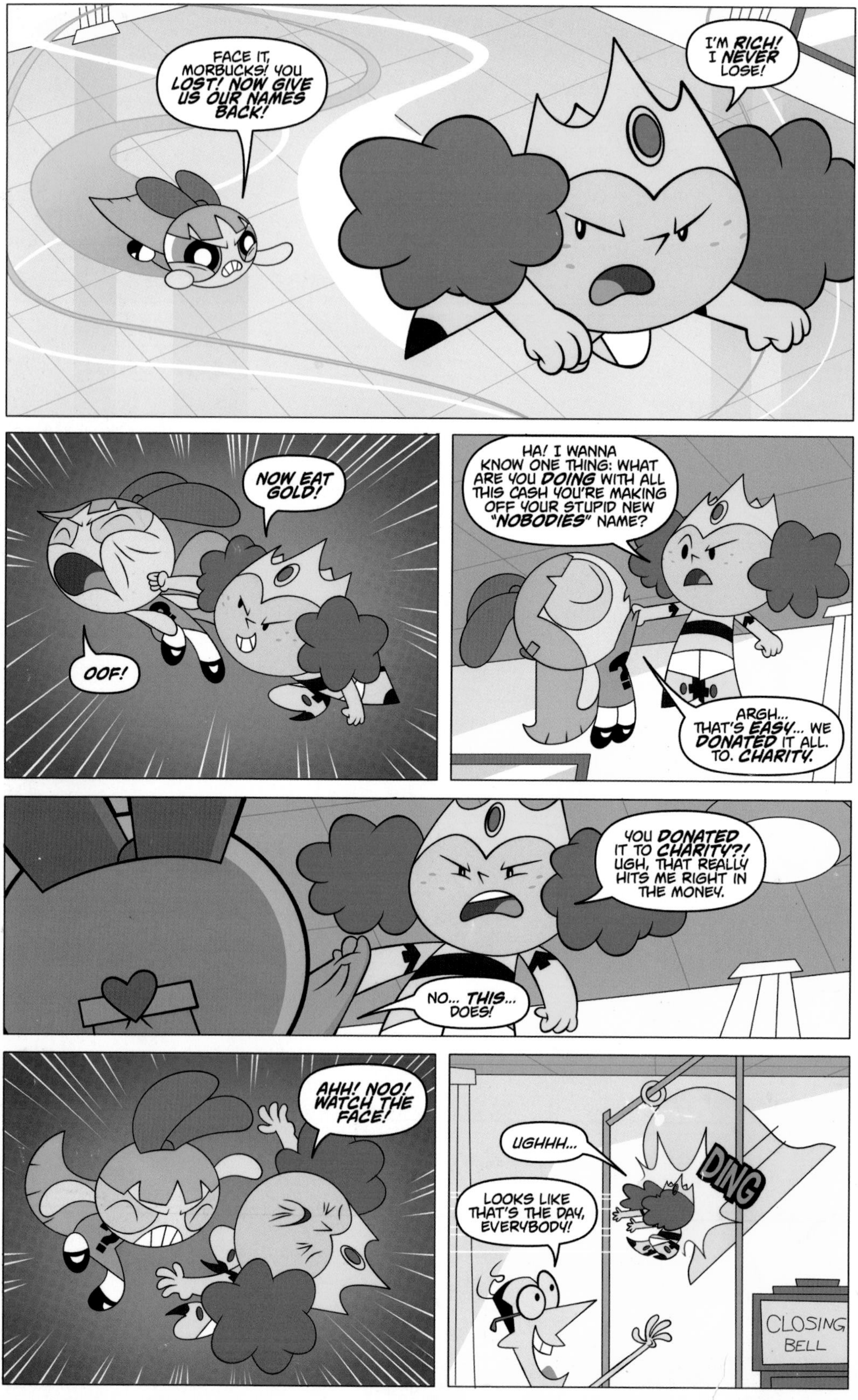
FACE IT, MORBUCKS! YOU LOST! NOW GIVE US OUR NAMES BACK!
I'M RICH! I NEVER LOSE!
NOW EAT GOLD!
OOF!
HA! I WANNA KNOW ONE THING: WHAT ARE YOU DOING WITH ALL THIS CASH YOU'RE MAKING OFF YOUR STUPID NEW "NOBODIES" NAME?
ARGH... THAT'S EASY... WE DONATED IT ALL. TO. CHARITY.
YOU DONATED IT TO CHARITY?! UGH, THAT REALLY HITS ME RIGHT IN THE MONEY.
NO... THIS... DOES!
AHH! NOO! WATCH THE FACE!
UGHHH...
DING
LOOKS LIKE THAT'S THE DAY, EVERYBODY!
CLOSING BELL

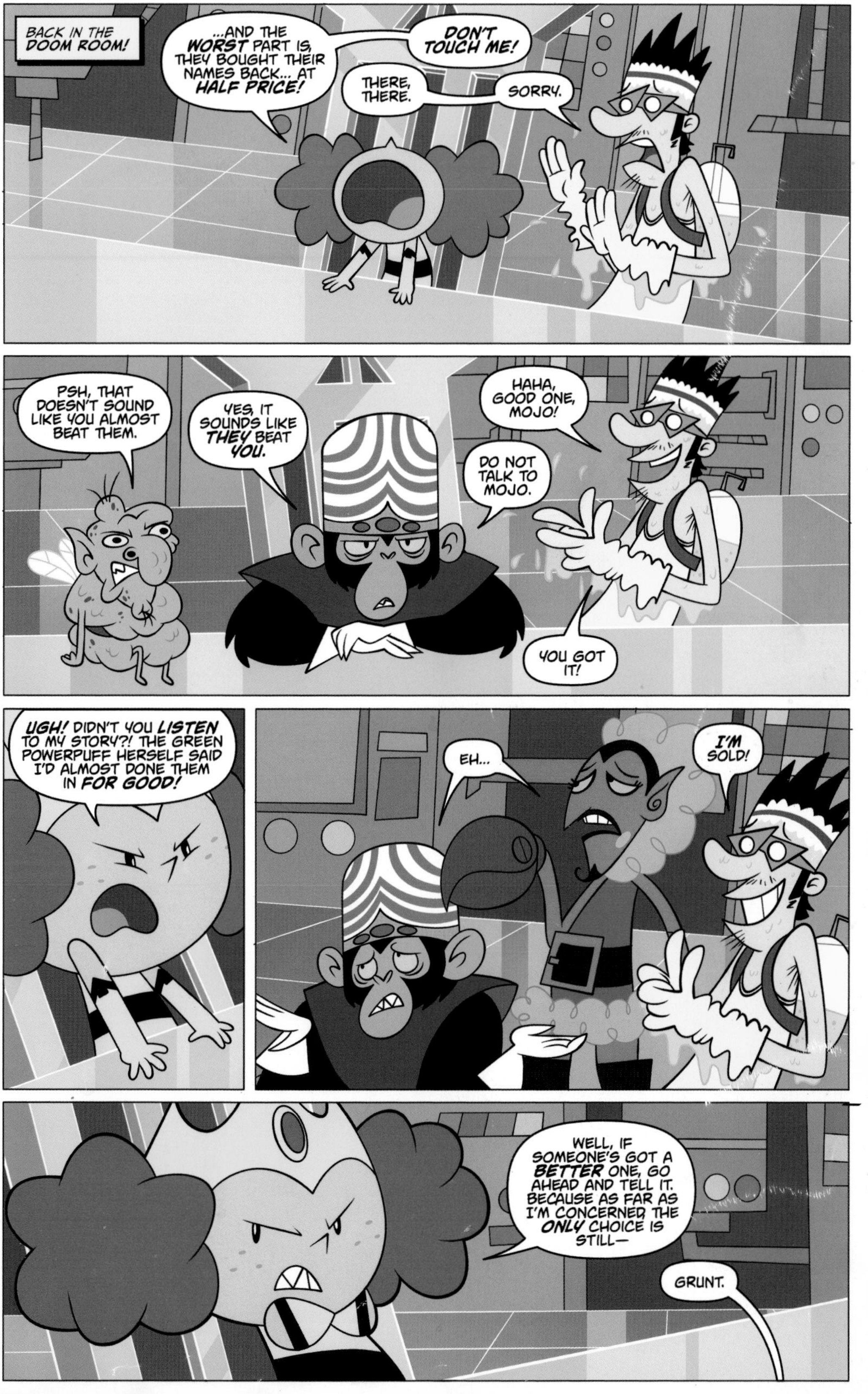
BACK IN THE DOOM ROOM!
...AND THE WORST PART IS, THEY BOUGHT THEIR NAMES BACK... AT HALF PRICE!
DON'T TOUCH ME!
THERE, THERE.
SORRY.
PSH, THAT DOESN'T SOUND LIKE YOU ALMOST BEAT THEM.
YES, IT SOUNDS LIKE THEY BEAT YOU.
HAHA, GOOD ONE, MOJO!
DO NOT TALK TO MOJO.
YOU GOT IT!
UGH! DIDN'T YOU LISTEN TO MY STORY?! THE GREEN POWERPUFF HERSELF SAID I'D ALMOST DONE THEM IN FOR GOOD!
EH...
I'M SOLD!
WELL, IF SOMEONE'S GOT A BETTER ONE, GO AHEAD AND TELL IT. BECAUSE AS FAR AS I'M CONCERNED, THE ONLY CHOICE IS STILL—
GRUNT.

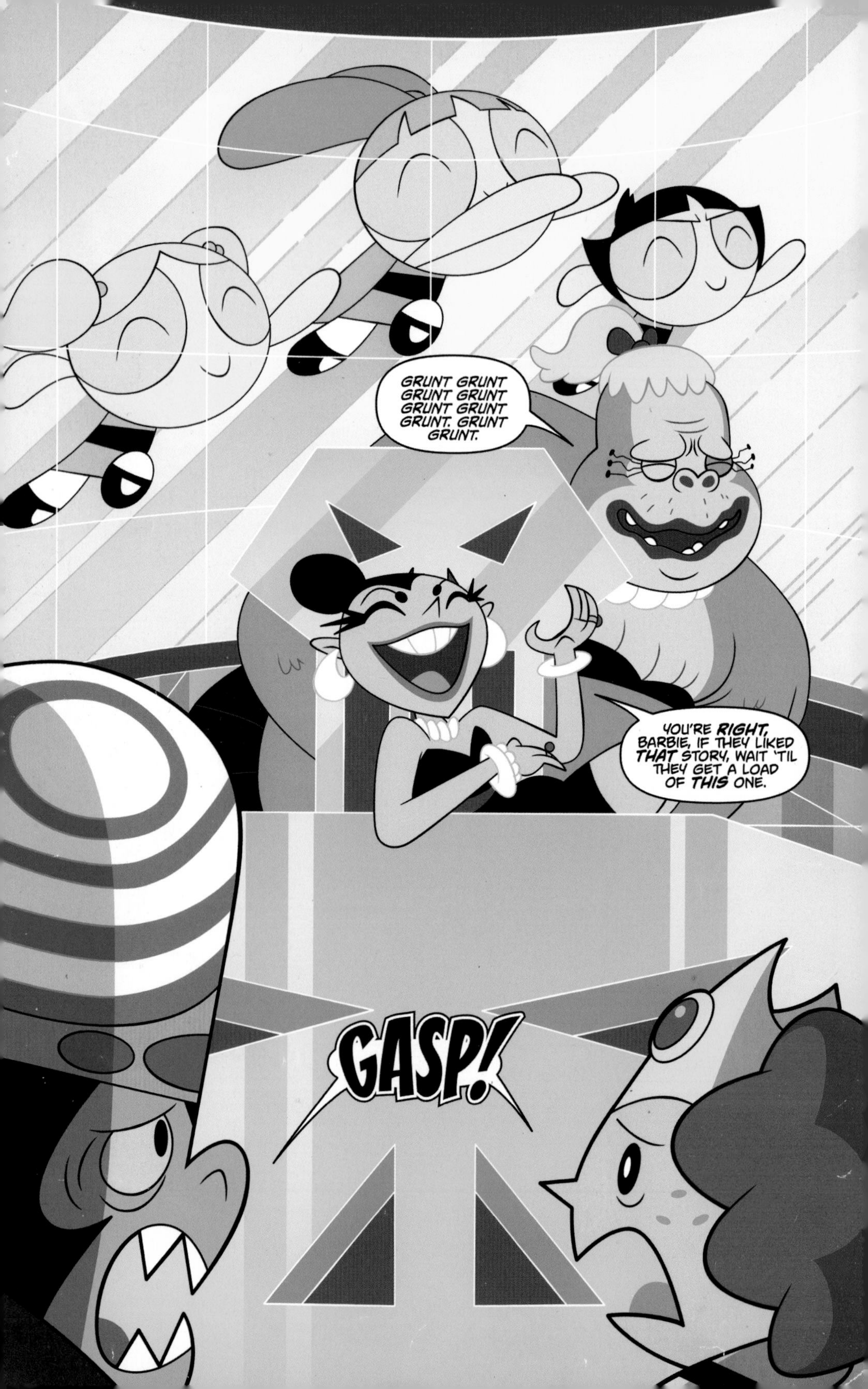
GRUNT GRUNT GRUNT GRUNT GRUNT GRUNT GRUNT. GRUNT GRUNT.
YOU'RE **RIGHT**, BARBIE, IF THEY LIKED **THAT** STORY, WAIT 'TIL THEY GET A LOAD OF **THIS** ONE.
GASP!

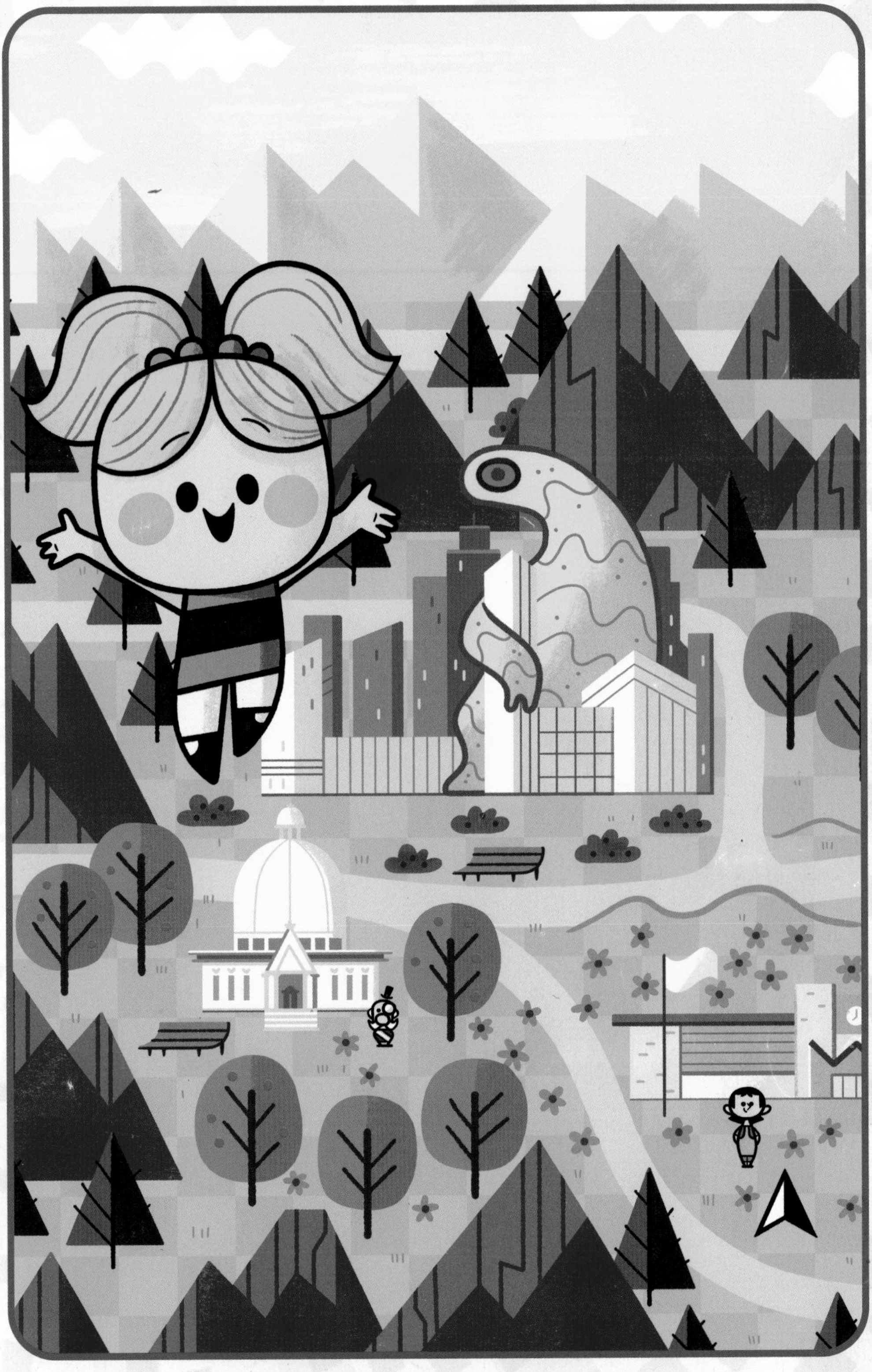

Cover Art by **Andrew Kolb**

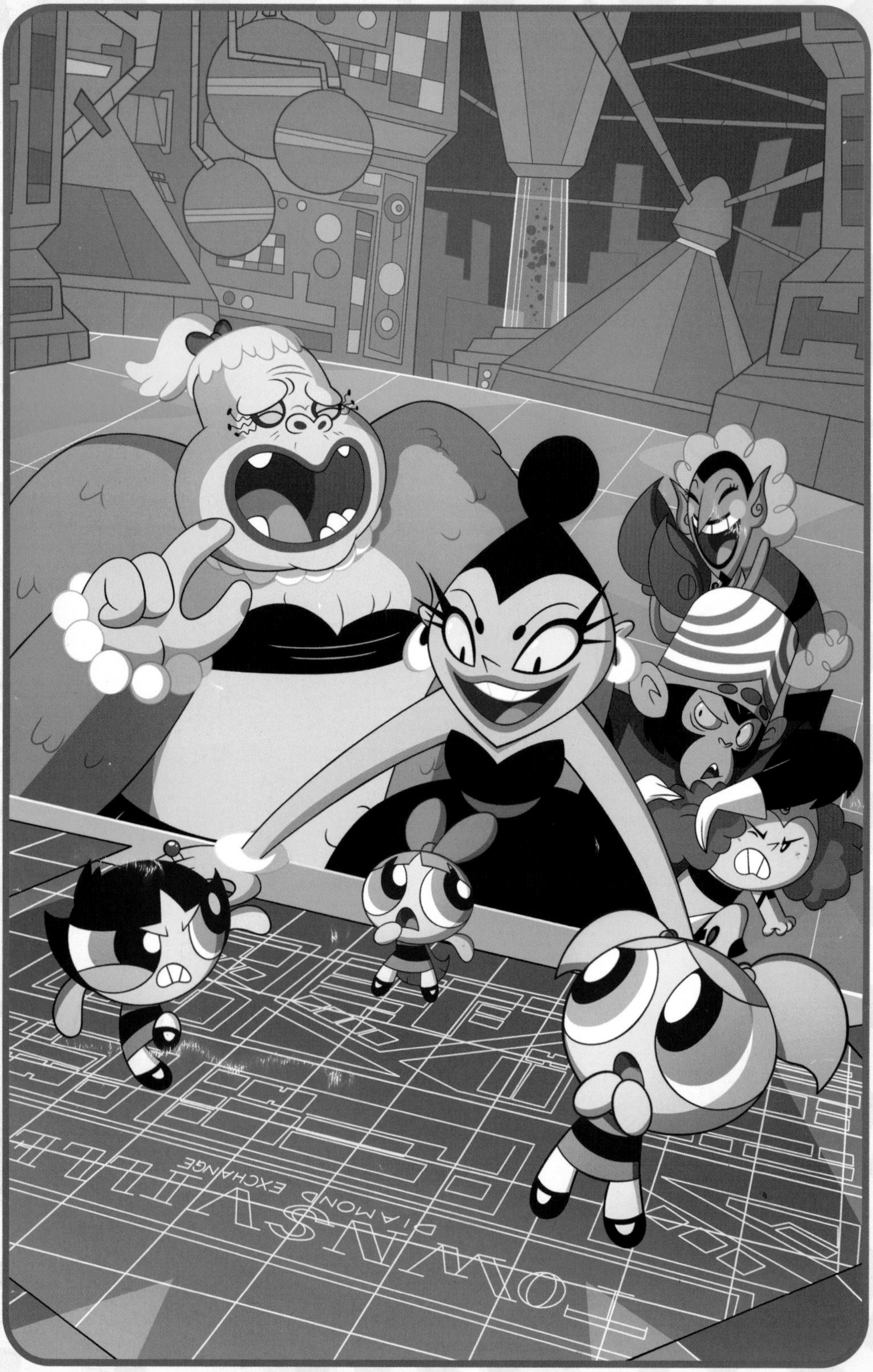
TOWNSVILLE
DIAMOND EXCHANGE

Cover Art by **Philip Murphy**

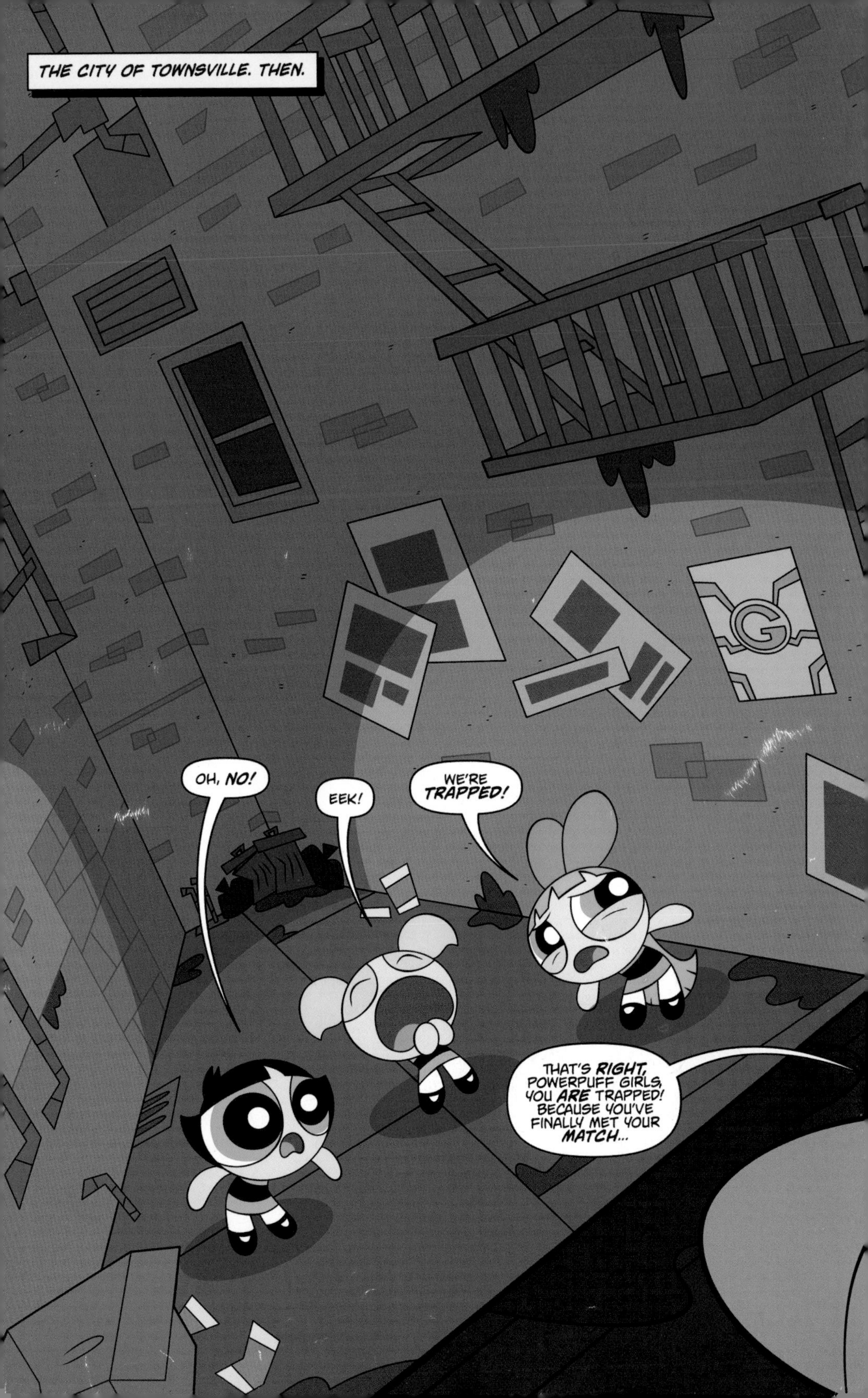
THE CITY OF TOWNSVILLE. THEN.
OH, NO!
EEK!
WE'RE TRAPPED!
THAT'S RIGHT, POWERPUFF GIRLS, YOU ARE TRAPPED! BECAUSE YOU'VE FINALLY MET YOUR MATCH...

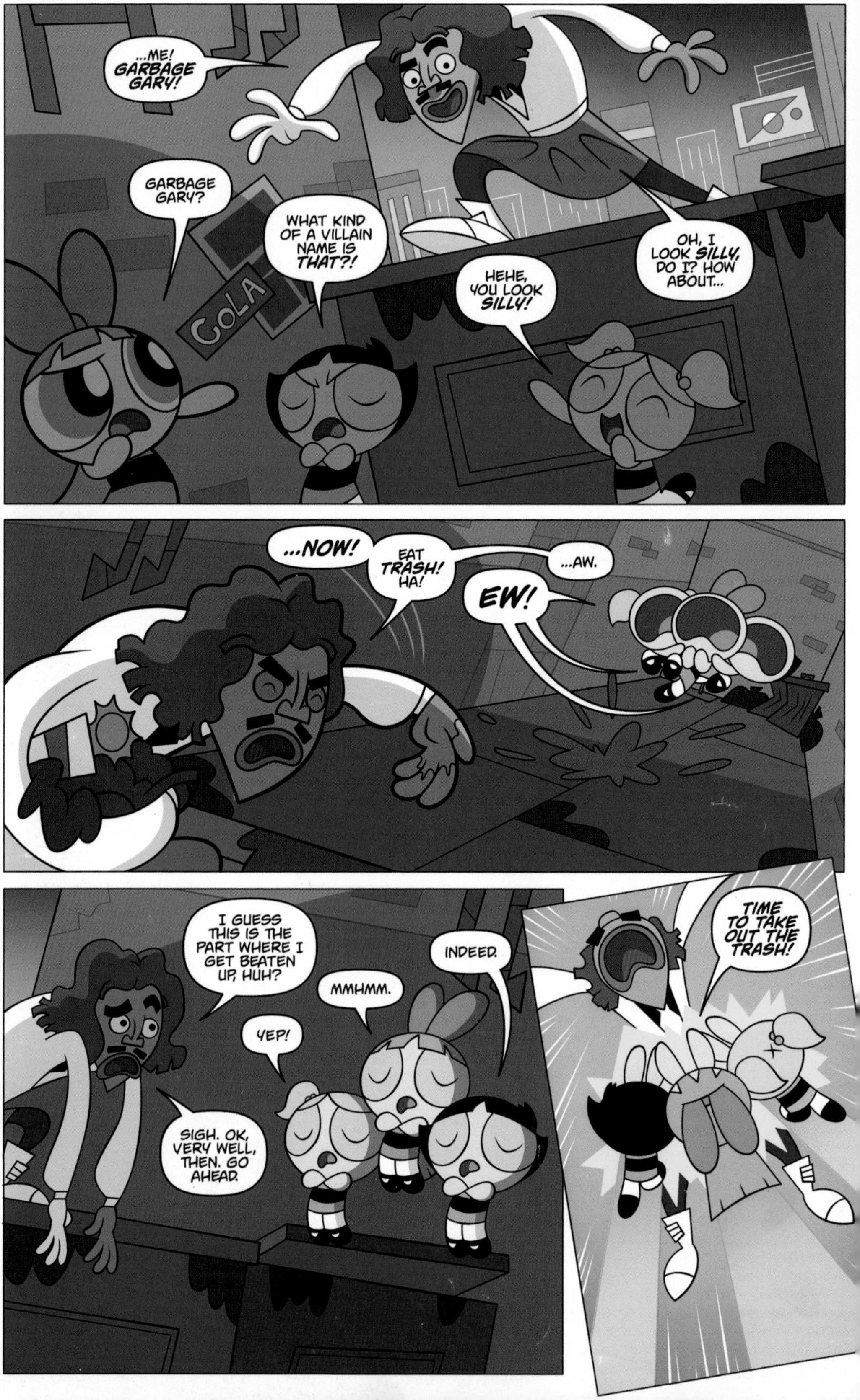
...ME! GARBAGE GARY!
GARBAGE GARY?
GOLA
WHAT KIND OF A VILLAIN NAME IS THAT?!
HEHE, YOU LOOK SILLY!
OH, I LOOK SILLY, DO I? HOW ABOUT...
...NOW!
EAT TRASH! HA!
...AW.
EW!
I GUESS THIS IS THE PART WHERE I GET BEATEN UP, HUH?
INDEED.
MMHMM.
YEP!
SIGH. OK, VERY WELL, THEN. GO AHEAD.
TIME TO TAKE OUT THE TRASH!

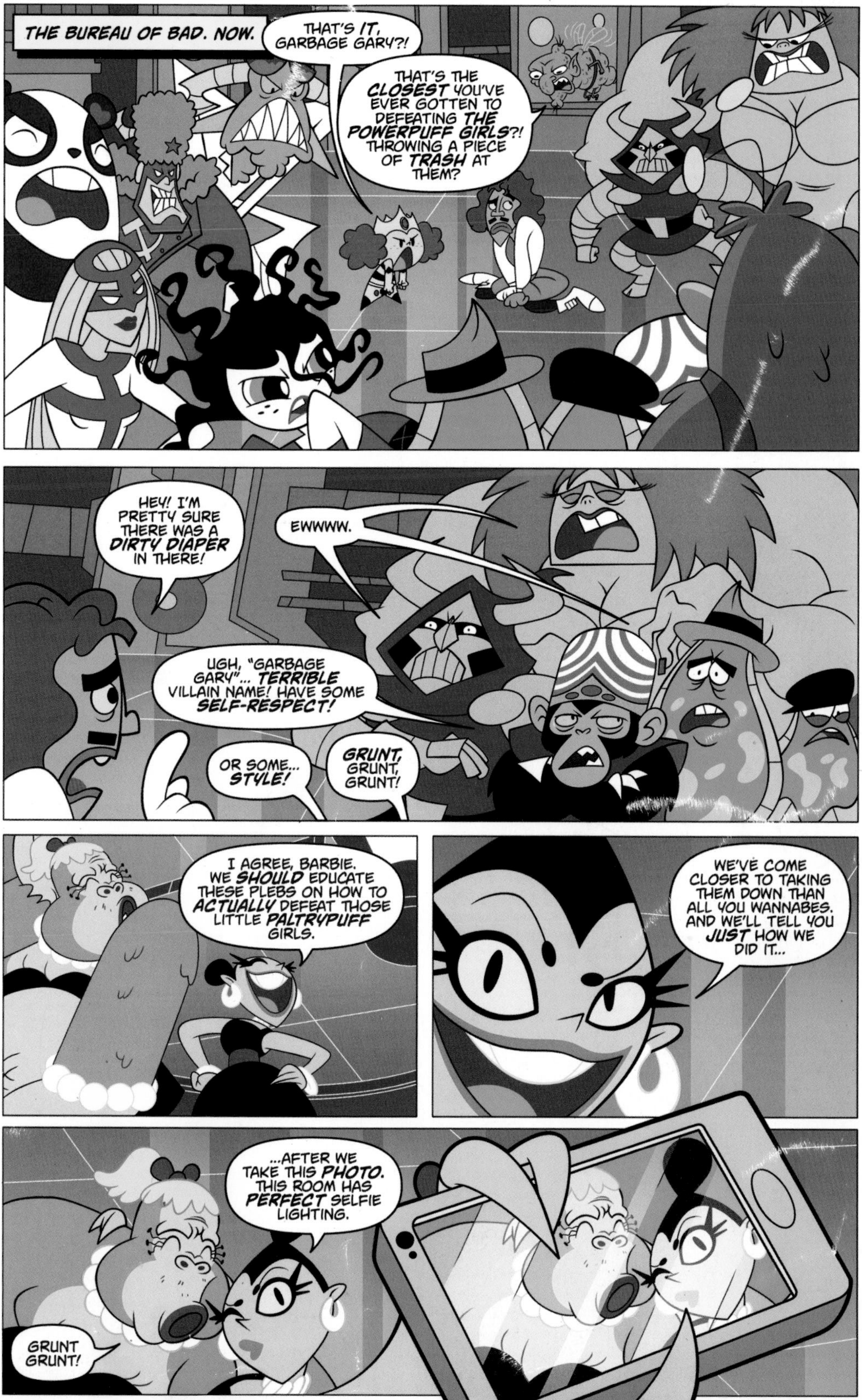
THE BUREAU OF BAD. NOW.
THAT'S IT, GARBAGE GARY?!
THAT'S THE CLOSEST YOU'VE EVER GOTTEN TO DEFEATING THE POWERPUFF GIRLS?! THROWING A PIECE OF TRASH AT THEM?
HEY! I'M PRETTY SURE THERE WAS A DIRTY DIAPER IN THERE!
EWWWW.
UGH, "GARBAGE GARY"... TERRIBLE VILLAIN NAME! HAVE SOME SELF-RESPECT!
OR SOME... STYLE!
GRUNT, GRUNT, GRUNT!
I AGREE, BARBIE. WE SHOULD EDUCATE THESE PLEBS ON HOW TO ACTUALLY DEFEAT THOSE LITTLE PALTRYPUFF GIRLS.
WE'VE COME CLOSER TO TAKING THEM DOWN THAN ALL YOU WANNABES. AND WE'LL TELL YOU JUST HOW WE DID IT...
...AFTER WE TAKE THIS PHOTO. THIS ROOM HAS PERFECT SELFIE LIGHTING.
GRUNT GRUNT!

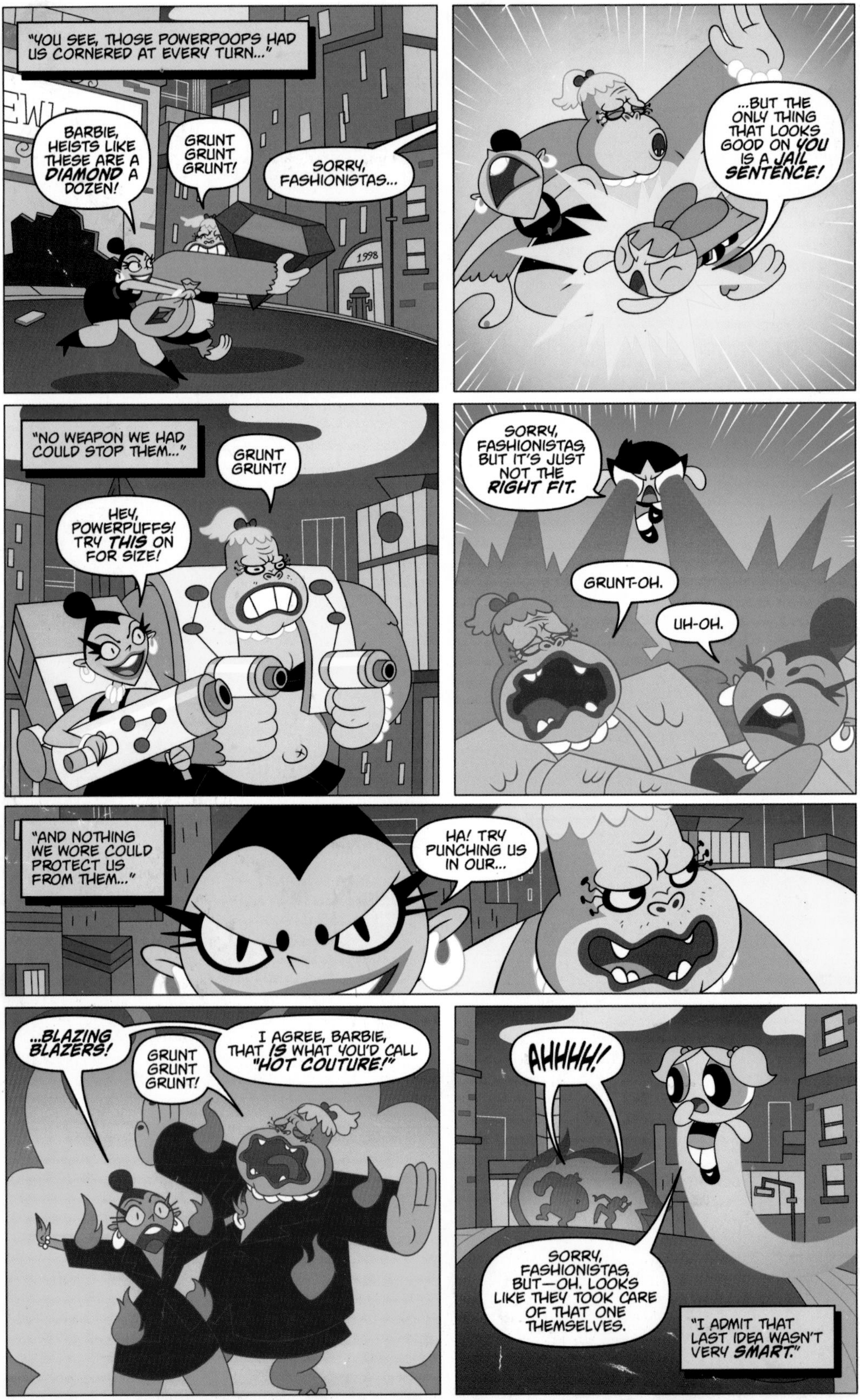
"YOU SEE, THOSE POWERPOOPS HAD US CORNERED AT EVERY TURN..."
BARBIE, HEISTS LIKE THESE ARE A DIAMOND A DOZEN!
GRUNT GRUNT GRUNT!
SORRY, FASHIONISTAS...
...BUT THE ONLY THING THAT LOOKS GOOD ON YOU IS A JAIL SENTENCE!
"NO WEAPON WE HAD COULD STOP THEM..."
GRUNT GRUNT!
HEY, POWERPUFFS! TRY THIS ON FOR SIZE!
SORRY, FASHIONISTAS, BUT IT'S JUST NOT THE RIGHT FIT.
GRUNT-OH.
UH-OH.
"AND NOTHING WE WORE COULD PROTECT US FROM THEM..."
HA! TRY PUNCHING US IN OUR...
...BLAZING BLAZERS!
GRUNT GRUNT GRUNT!
I AGREE, BARBIE, THAT IS WHAT YOU'D CALL "HOT COUTURE!"
AHHHH!
SORRY, FASHIONISTAS, BUT—OH. LOOKS LIKE THEY TOOK CARE OF THAT ONE THEMSELVES.
"I ADMIT THAT LAST IDEA WASN'T VERY SMART."

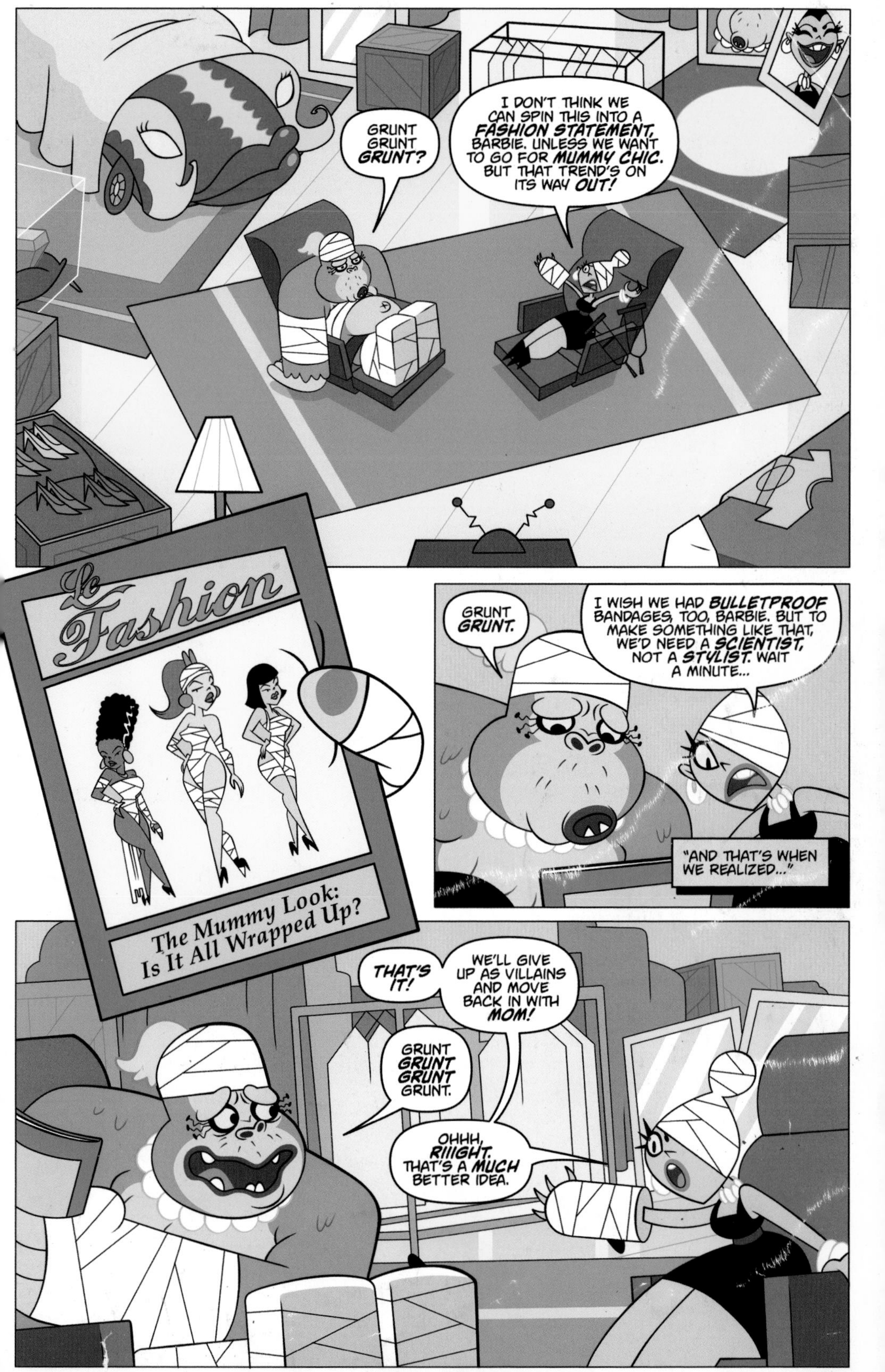
GRUNT GRUNT GRUNT?
I DON'T THINK WE CAN SPIN THIS INTO A FASHION STATEMENT, BARBIE. UNLESS WE WANT TO GO FOR MUMMY CHIC. BUT THAT TREND'S ON ITS WAY OUT!
Le Fashion
The Mummy Look: Is It All Wrapped Up?
GRUNT GRUNT.
I WISH WE HAD BULLETPROOF BANDAGES, TOO, BARBIE. BUT TO MAKE SOMETHING LIKE THAT, WE'D NEED A SCIENTIST, NOT A STYLIST. WAIT A MINUTE...
"AND THAT'S WHEN WE REALIZED..."
THAT'S IT!
WE'LL GIVE UP AS VILLAINS AND MOVE BACK IN WITH MOM!
GRUNT GRUNT GRUNT GRUNT.
OHHH, RIIIGHT. THAT'S A MUCH BETTER IDEA.

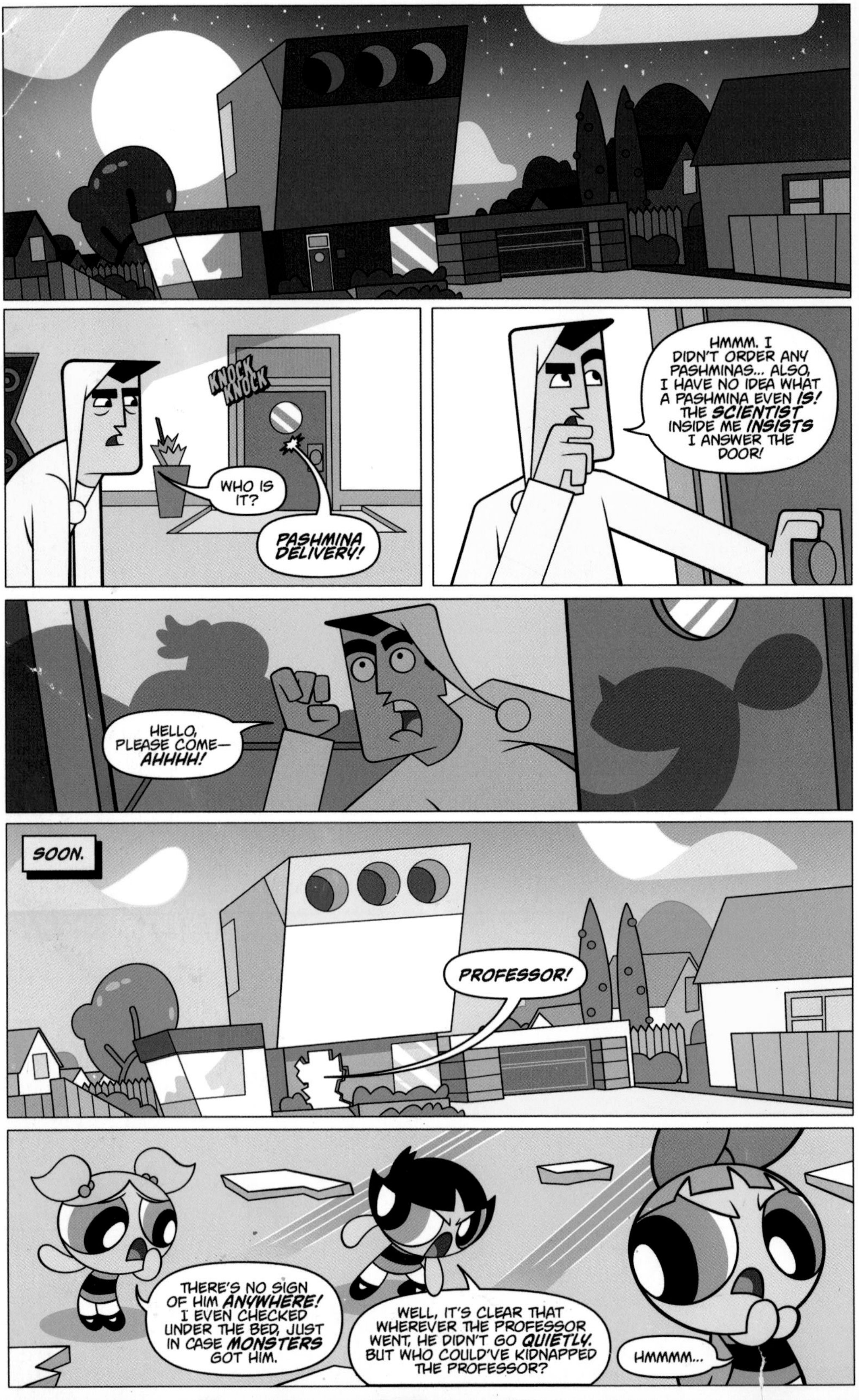
KNOCK KNOCK
WHO IS IT?
PASHMINA DELIVERY!
HMMM. I DIDN'T ORDER ANY PASHMINAS... ALSO, I HAVE NO IDEA WHAT A PASHMINA EVEN IS! THE SCIENTIST INSIDE ME INSISTS I ANSWER THE DOOR!
HELLO, PLEASE COME— AHHHH!
SOON.
PROFESSOR!
THERE'S NO SIGN OF HIM ANYWHERE! I EVEN CHECKED UNDER THE BED, JUST IN CASE MONSTERS GOT HIM.
WELL, IT'S CLEAR THAT WHEREVER THE PROFESSOR WENT, HE DIDN'T GO QUIETLY. BUT WHO COULD'VE KIDNAPPED THE PROFESSOR?
HMMMM...

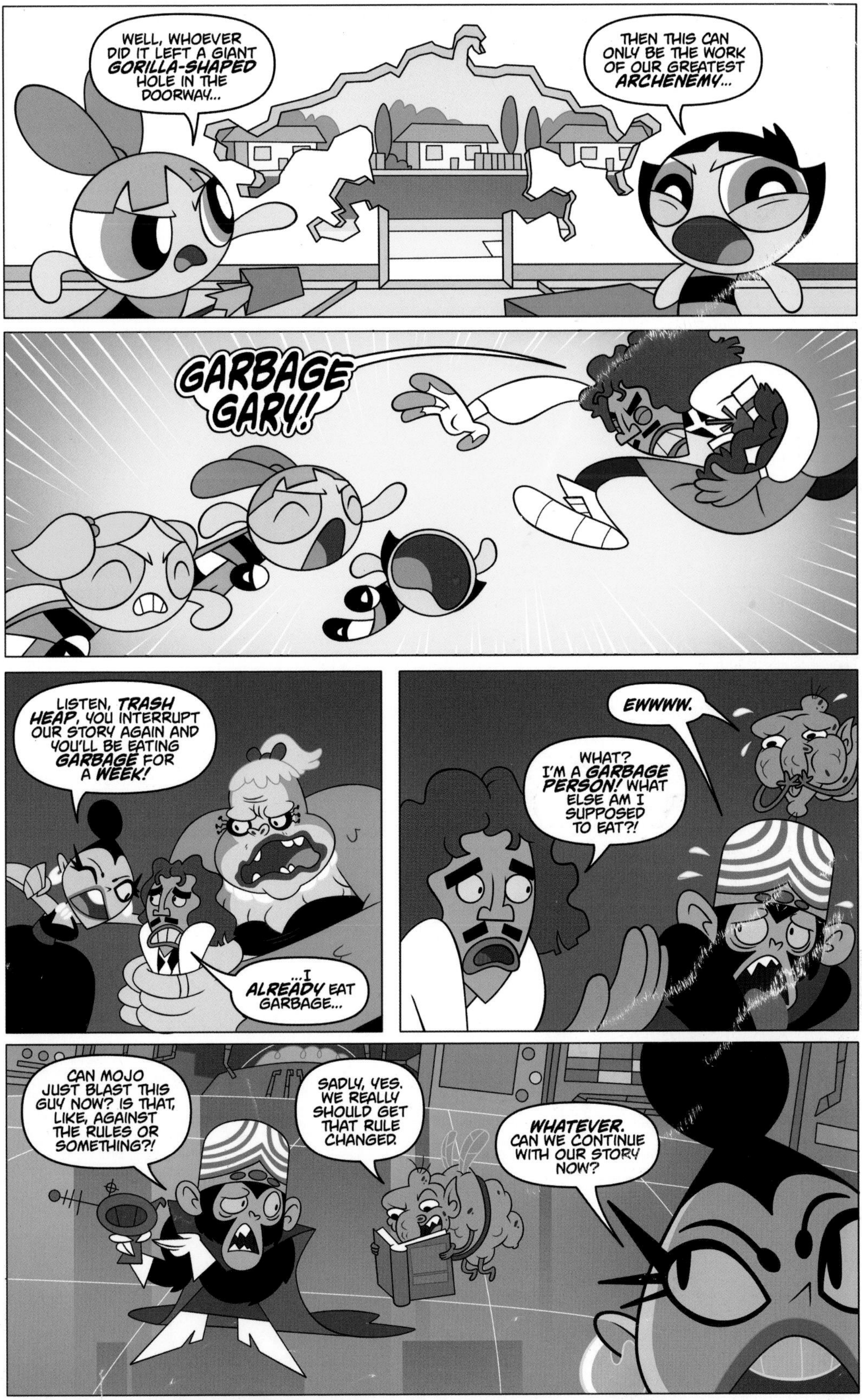
WELL, WHOEVER DID IT LEFT A GIANT GORILLA-SHAPED HOLE IN THE DOORWAY...
THEN THIS CAN ONLY BE THE WORK OF OUR GREATEST ARCHENEMY...
GARBAGE GARY!
LISTEN, TRASH HEAP, YOU INTERRUPT OUR STORY AGAIN AND YOU'LL BE EATING GARBAGE FOR A WEEK!
...I ALREADY EAT GARBAGE...
EWWWW.
WHAT? I'M A GARBAGE PERSON! WHAT ELSE AM I SUPPOSED TO EAT?!
CAN MOJO JUST BLAST THIS GUY NOW? IS THAT, LIKE, AGAINST THE RULES OR SOMETHING?!
SADLY, YES. WE REALLY SHOULD GET THAT RULE CHANGED.
WHATEVER. CAN WE CONTINUE WITH OUR STORY NOW?

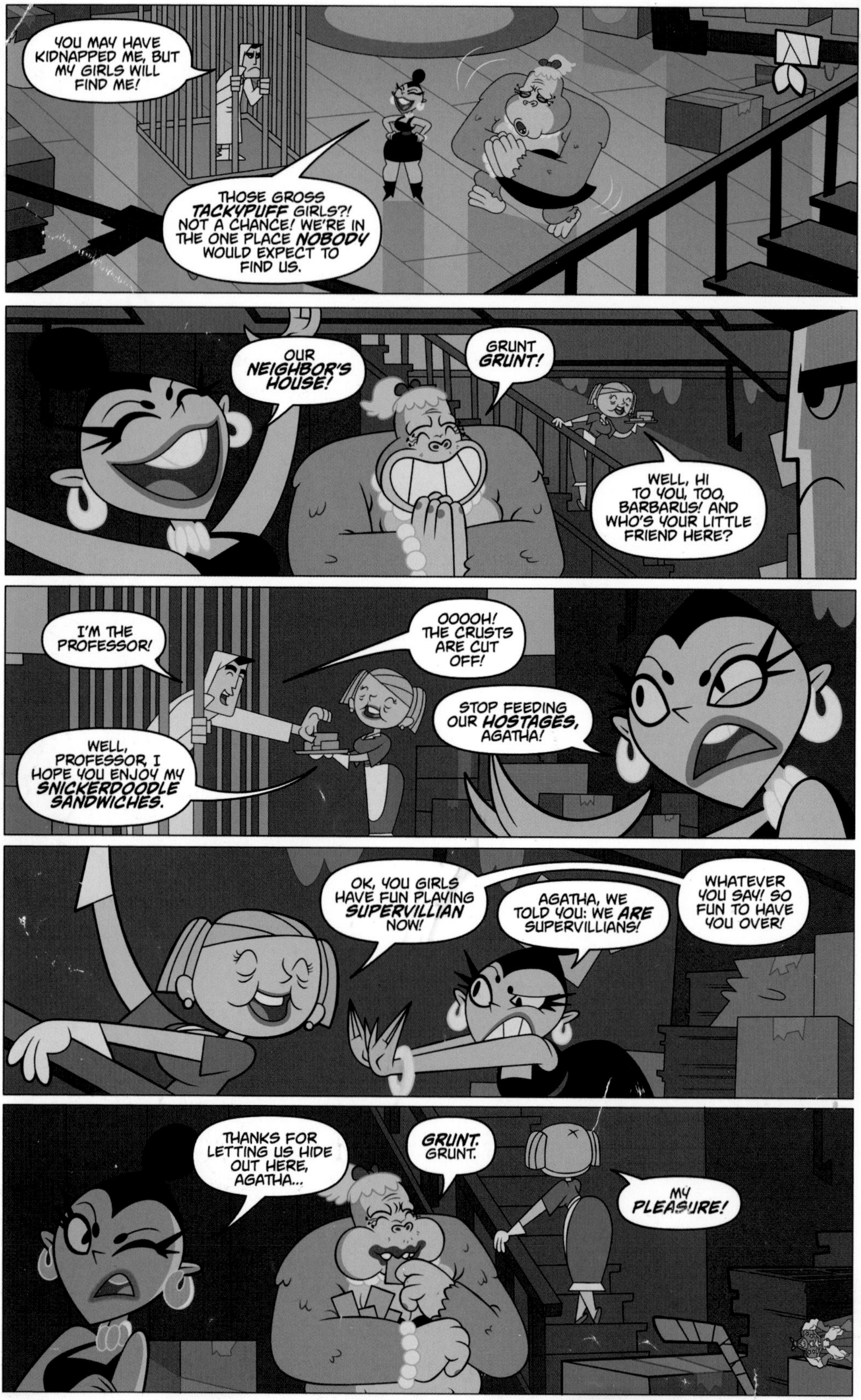
YOU MAY HAVE KIDNAPPED ME, BUT MY GIRLS WILL FIND ME!
THOSE GROSS TACKYPUFF GIRLS?! NOT A CHANCE! WE'RE IN THE ONE PLACE NOBODY WOULD EXPECT TO FIND US.
OUR NEIGHBOR'S HOUSE!
GRUNT GRUNT!
WELL, HI TO YOU, TOO, BARBARUS! AND WHO'S YOUR LITTLE FRIEND HERE?
I'M THE PROFESSOR!
WELL, PROFESSOR, I HOPE YOU ENJOY MY SNICKERDOODLE SANDWICHES.
OOOOH! THE CRUSTS ARE CUT OFF!
STOP FEEDING OUR HOSTAGES, AGATHA!
OK, YOU GIRLS HAVE FUN PLAYING SUPERVILLIAN NOW!
AGATHA, WE TOLD YOU: WE ARE SUPERVILLIANS!
WHATEVER YOU SAY! SO FUN TO HAVE YOU OVER!
THANKS FOR LETTING US HIDE OUT HERE, AGATHA...
GRUNT. GRUNT.
MY PLEASURE!

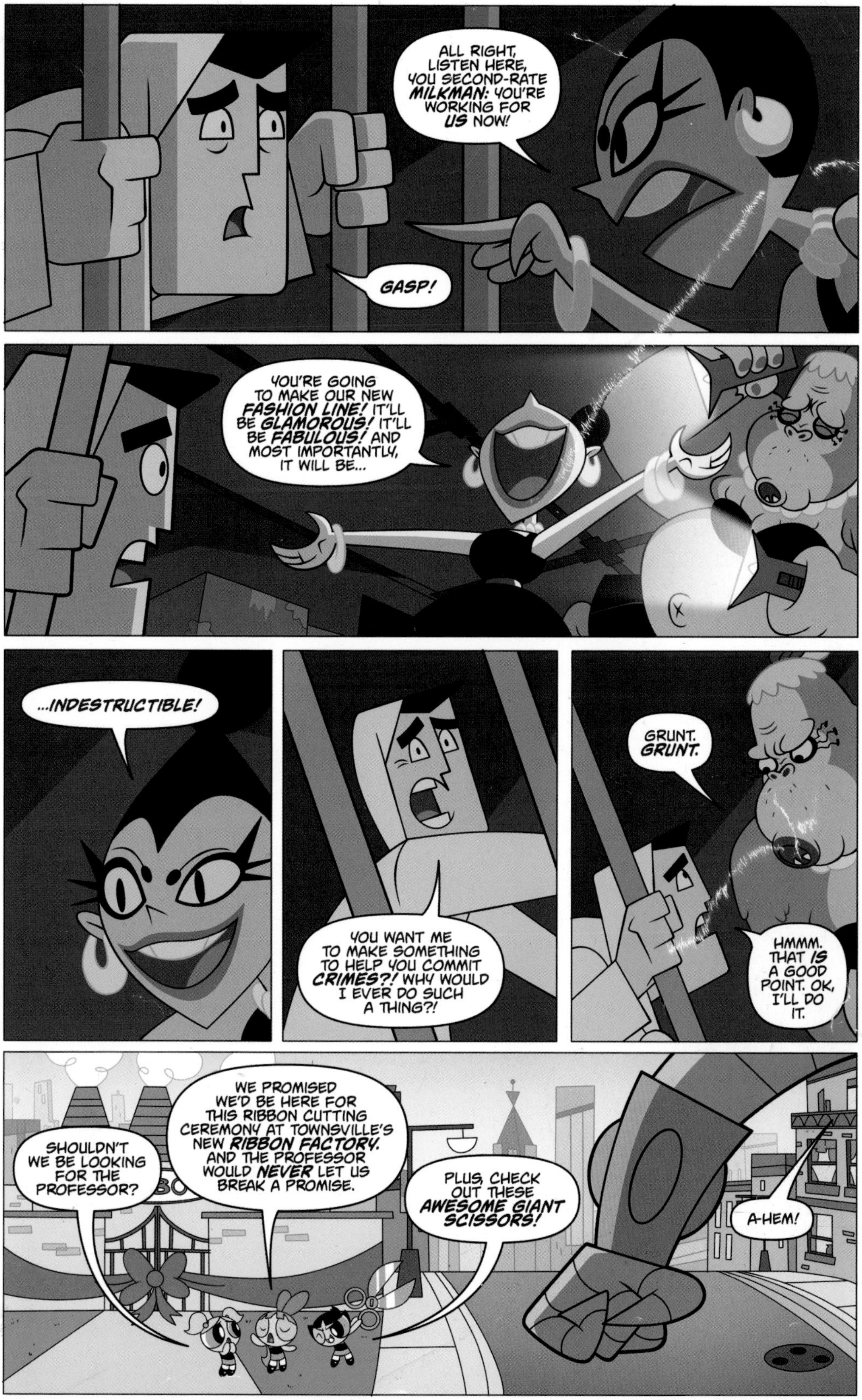
ALL RIGHT, LISTEN HERE, YOU SECOND-RATE MILKMAN: YOU'RE WORKING FOR US NOW!
GASP!
YOU'RE GOING TO MAKE OUR NEW FASHION LINE! IT'LL BE GLAMOROUS! IT'LL BE FABULOUS! AND MOST IMPORTANTLY, IT WILL BE...
...INDESTRUCTIBLE!
YOU WANT ME TO MAKE SOMETHING TO HELP YOU COMMIT CRIMES?! WHY WOULD I EVER DO SUCH A THING?!
GRUNT. GRUNT.
HMMM. THAT IS A GOOD POINT. OK, I'LL DO IT.
SHOULDN'T WE BE LOOKING FOR THE PROFESSOR?
WE PROMISED WE'D BE HERE FOR THIS RIBBON CUTTING CEREMONY AT TOWNSVILLE'S NEW RIBBON FACTORY. AND THE PROFESSOR WOULD NEVER LET US BREAK A PROMISE.
PLUS, CHECK OUT THESE AWESOME GIANT SCISSORS!
A-HEM!

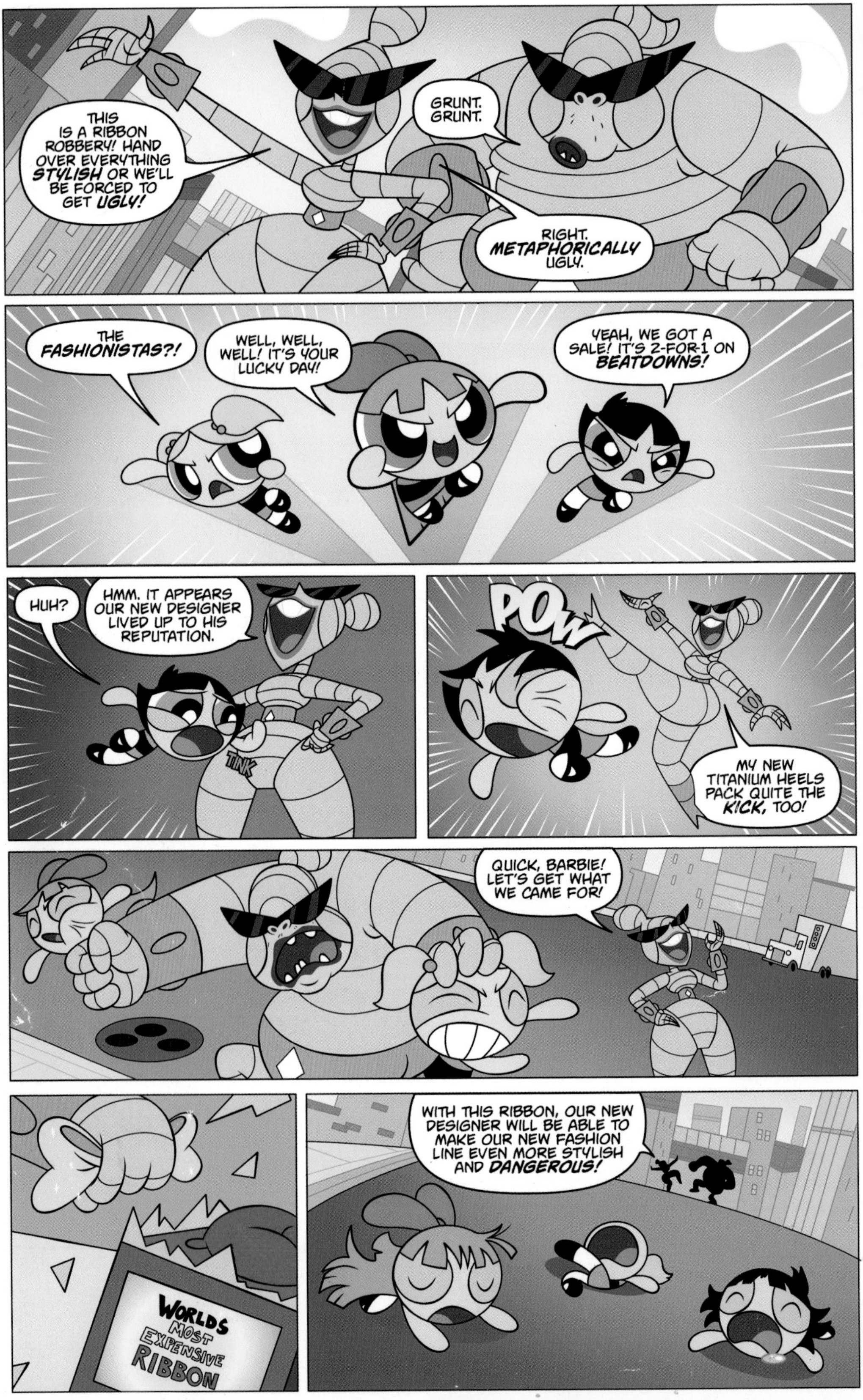
THIS IS A RIBBON ROBBERY! HAND OVER EVERYTHING STYLISH OR WE'LL BE FORCED TO GET UGLY!
GRUNT. GRUNT.
RIGHT. METAPHORICALLY UGLY.
THE FASHIONISTAS?!
WELL, WELL, WELL! IT'S YOUR LUCKY DAY!
YEAH, WE GOT A SALE! IT'S 2-FOR-1 ON BEATDOWNS!
HUH?
HMM. IT APPEARS OUR NEW DESIGNER LIVED UP TO HIS REPUTATION.
TINK
POW
MY NEW TITANIUM HEELS PACK QUITE THE KICK, TOO!
QUICK, BARBIE! LET'S GET WHAT WE CAME FOR!
WORLDS MOST EXPENSIVE RIBBON
WITH THIS RIBBON, OUR NEW DESIGNER WILL BE ABLE TO MAKE OUR NEW FASHION LINE EVEN MORE STYLISH AND DANGEROUS!

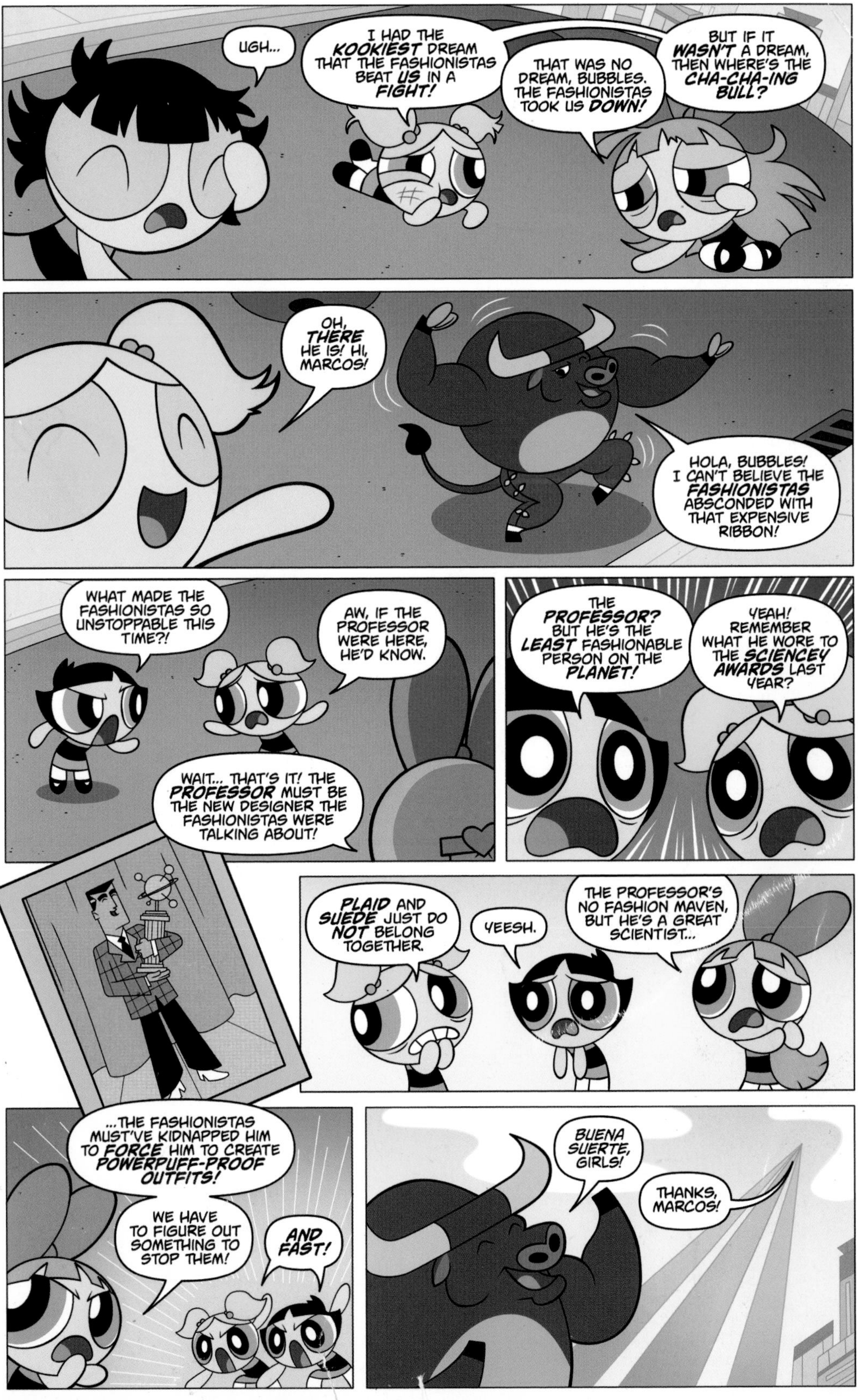
UGH...
I HAD THE KOOKIEST DREAM THAT THE FASHIONISTAS BEAT US IN A FIGHT!
THAT WAS NO DREAM, BUBBLES. THE FASHIONISTAS TOOK US DOWN!
BUT IF IT WASN'T A DREAM, THEN WHERE'S THE CHA-CHA-ING BULL?
OH, THERE HE IS! HI, MARCOS!
HOLA, BUBBLES! I CAN'T BELIEVE THE FASHIONISTAS ABSCONDED WITH THAT EXPENSIVE RIBBON!
WHAT MADE THE FASHIONISTAS SO UNSTOPPABLE THIS TIME?!
AW, IF THE PROFESSOR WERE HERE, HE'D KNOW.
WAIT... THAT'S IT! THE PROFESSOR MUST BE THE NEW DESIGNER THE FASHIONISTAS WERE TALKING ABOUT!
THE PROFESSOR? BUT HE'S THE LEAST FASHIONABLE PERSON ON THE PLANET!
YEAH! REMEMBER WHAT HE WORE TO THE SCIENCEY AWARDS LAST YEAR?
PLAID AND SUEDE JUST DO NOT BELONG TOGETHER.
YEESH.
THE PROFESSOR'S NO FASHION MAVEN, BUT HE'S A GREAT SCIENTIST...
...THE FASHIONISTAS MUST'VE KIDNAPPED HIM TO FORCE HIM TO CREATE POWERPUFF-PROOF OUTFITS!
WE HAVE TO FIGURE OUT SOMETHING TO STOP THEM!
AND FAST!
BUENA SUERTE, GIRLS!
THANKS, MARCOS!

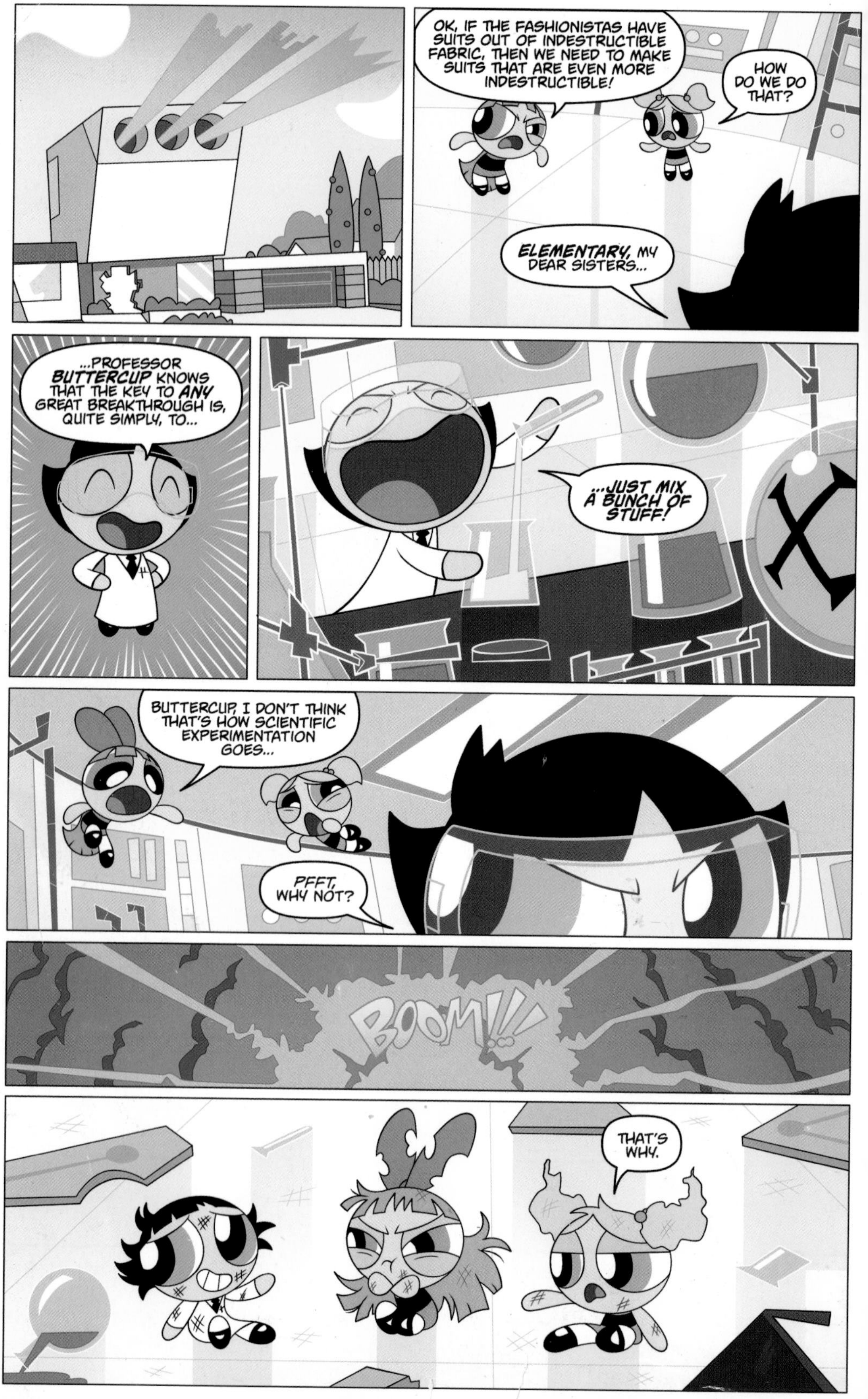
OK, IF THE FASHIONISTAS HAVE SUITS OUT OF INDESTRUCTIBLE FABRIC, THEN WE NEED TO MAKE SUITS THAT ARE EVEN MORE INDESTRUCTIBLE!
HOW DO WE DO THAT?
ELEMENTARY, MY DEAR SISTERS...
...PROFESSOR BUTTERCUP KNOWS THAT THE KEY TO ANY GREAT BREAKTHROUGH IS, QUITE SIMPLY, TO...
...JUST MIX A BUNCH OF STUFF!
BUTTERCUP, I DON'T THINK THAT'S HOW SCIENTIFIC EXPERIMENTATION GOES...
PFFT, WHY NOT?
BOOM!!!
THAT'S WHY.

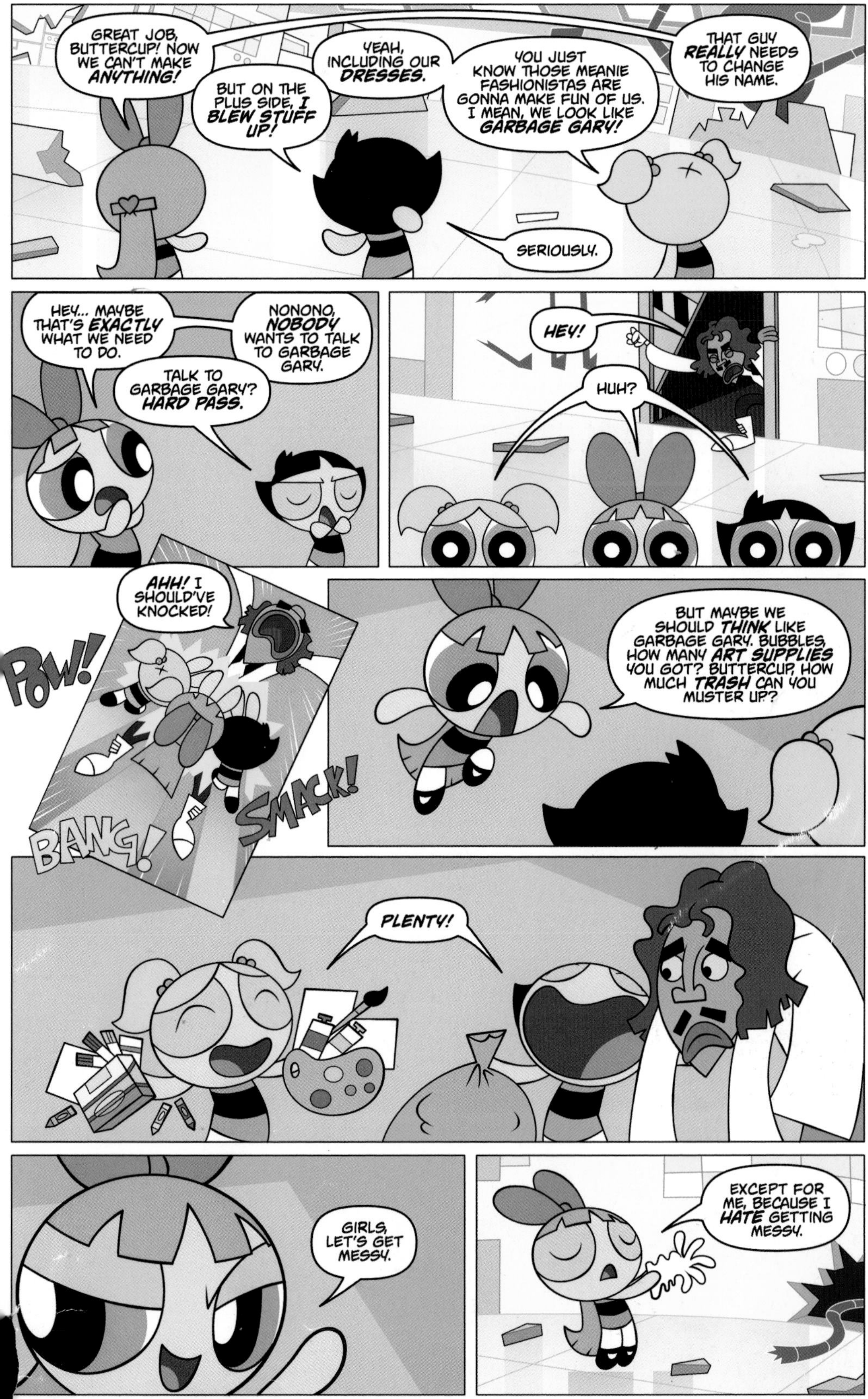
GREAT JOB, BUTTERCUP! NOW WE CAN'T MAKE ANYTHING!
BUT ON THE PLUS SIDE, I BLEW STUFF UP!
YEAH, INCLUDING OUR DRESSES.
YOU JUST KNOW THOSE MEANIE FASHIONISTAS ARE GONNA MAKE FUN OF US. I MEAN, WE LOOK LIKE GARBAGE GARY!
THAT GUY REALLY NEEDS TO CHANGE HIS NAME.
SERIOUSLY.
HEY... MAYBE THAT'S EXACTLY WHAT WE NEED TO DO.
NONONO, NOBODY WANTS TO TALK TO GARBAGE GARY.
TALK TO GARBAGE GARY? HARD PASS.
HEY!
HUH?
AHH! I SHOULD'VE KNOCKED!
POW!
SMACK!
BANG!
BUT MAYBE WE SHOULD THINK LIKE GARBAGE GARY. BUBBLES, HOW MANY ART SUPPLIES YOU GOT? BUTTERCUP, HOW MUCH TRASH CAN YOU MUSTER UP?
PLENTY!
GIRLS, LET'S GET MESSY.
EXCEPT FOR ME, BECAUSE I HATE GETTING MESSY.

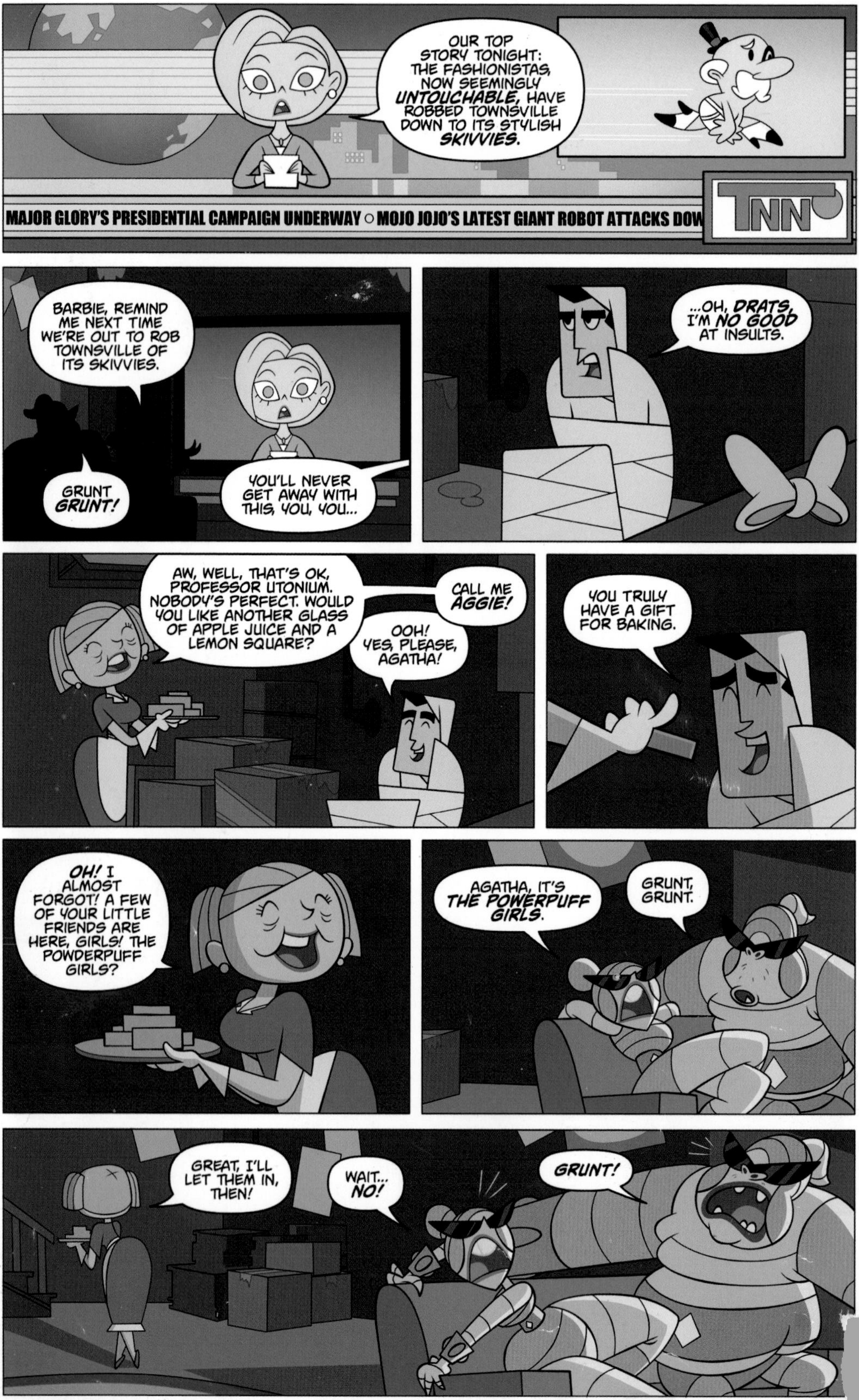

OUR TOP STORY TONIGHT: THE FASHIONISTAS, NOW SEEMINGLY UNTOUCHABLE, HAVE ROBBED TOWNSVILLE DOWN TO ITS STYLISH SKIVVIES.
MAJOR GLORY'S PRESIDENTIAL CAMPAIGN UNDERWAY ○ MOJO JOJO'S LATEST GIANT ROBOT ATTACKS DOW
TNN
BARBIE, REMIND ME NEXT TIME WE'RE OUT TO ROB TOWNSVILLE OF ITS SKIVVIES.
GRUNT GRUNT!
YOU'LL NEVER GET AWAY WITH THIS, YOU, YOU...
...OH, DRATS, I'M NO GOOD AT INSULTS.
AW, WELL, THAT'S OK, PROFESSOR UTONIUM. NOBODY'S PERFECT. WOULD YOU LIKE ANOTHER GLASS OF APPLE JUICE AND A LEMON SQUARE?
CALL ME AGGIE!
OOH! YES, PLEASE, AGATHA!
YOU TRULY HAVE A GIFT FOR BAKING.
OH! I ALMOST FORGOT! A FEW OF YOUR LITTLE FRIENDS ARE HERE, GIRLS! THE POWDERPUFF GIRLS?
AGATHA, IT'S THE POWERPUFF GIRLS.
GRUNT, GRUNT.
GREAT, I'LL LET THEM IN, THEN!
WAIT... NO!
GRUNT!

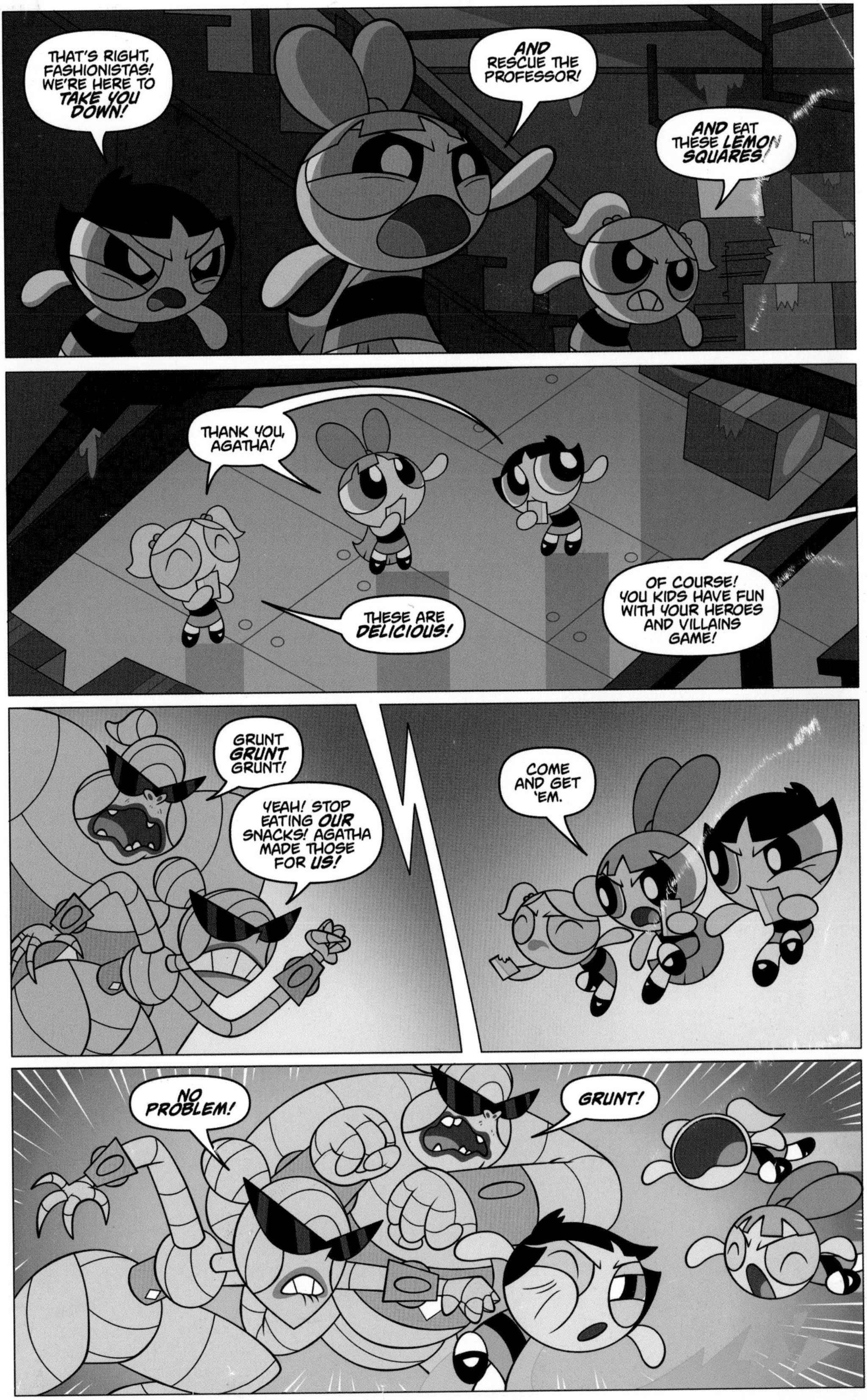

THAT'S RIGHT, FASHIONISTAS! WE'RE HERE TO TAKE YOU DOWN!
AND RESCUE THE PROFESSOR!
AND EAT THESE LEMON SQUARES!
THANK YOU, AGATHA!
THESE ARE DELICIOUS!
OF COURSE! YOU KIDS HAVE FUN WITH YOUR HEROES AND VILLAINS GAME!
GRUNT GRUNT GRUNT!
YEAH! STOP EATING OUR SNACKS! AGATHA MADE THOSE FOR US!
COME AND GET 'EM.
NO PROBLEM!
GRUNT!

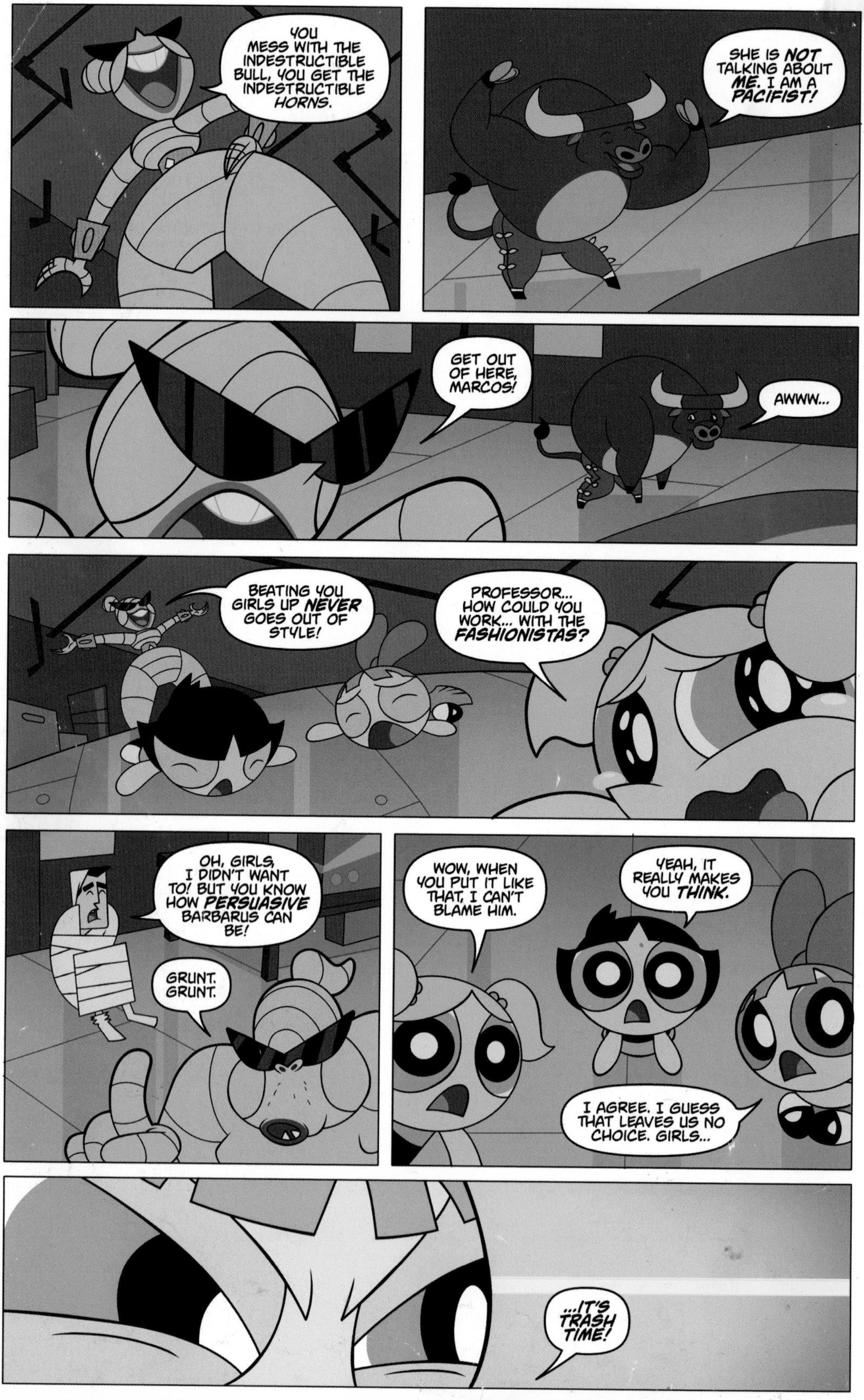
YOU MESS WITH THE INDESTRUCTIBLE BULL, YOU GET THE INDESTRUCTIBLE HORNS.
SHE IS NOT TALKING ABOUT ME. I AM A PACIFIST!
GET OUT OF HERE, MARCOS!
AWWW...
BEATING YOU GIRLS UP NEVER GOES OUT OF STYLE!
PROFESSOR... HOW COULD YOU WORK... WITH THE FASHIONISTAS?
OH, GIRLS, I DIDN'T WANT TO! BUT YOU KNOW HOW PERSUASIVE BARBARUS CAN BE!
GRUNT. GRUNT.
WOW, WHEN YOU PUT IT LIKE THAT, I CAN'T BLAME HIM.
YEAH, IT REALLY MAKES YOU THINK.
I AGREE. I GUESS THAT LEAVES US NO CHOICE. GIRLS...
...IT'S TRASH TIME!

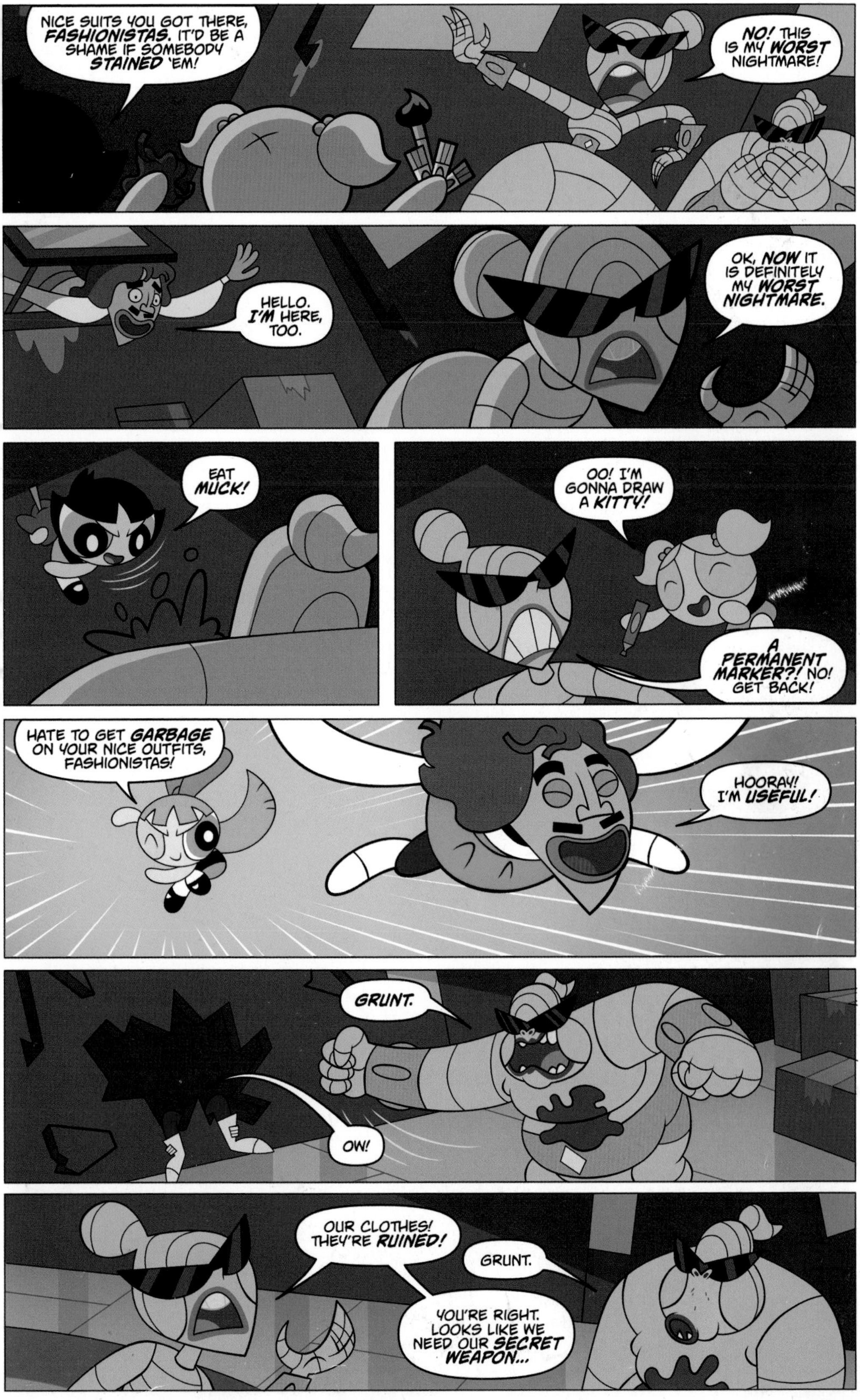
NICE SUITS YOU GOT THERE, FASHIONISTAS. IT'D BE A SHAME IF SOMEBODY STAINED 'EM!
NO! THIS IS MY WORST NIGHTMARE!
HELLO. I'M HERE, TOO.
OK, NOW IT IS DEFINITELY MY WORST NIGHTMARE.
EAT MUCK!
OO! I'M GONNA DRAW A KITTY!
A PERMANENT MARKER?! NO! GET BACK!
HATE TO GET GARBAGE ON YOUR NICE OUTFITS, FASHIONISTAS!
HOORAY! I'M USEFUL!
GRUNT.
OW!
OUR CLOTHES! THEY'RE RUINED!
GRUNT.
YOU'RE RIGHT. LOOKS LIKE WE NEED OUR SECRET WEAPON...

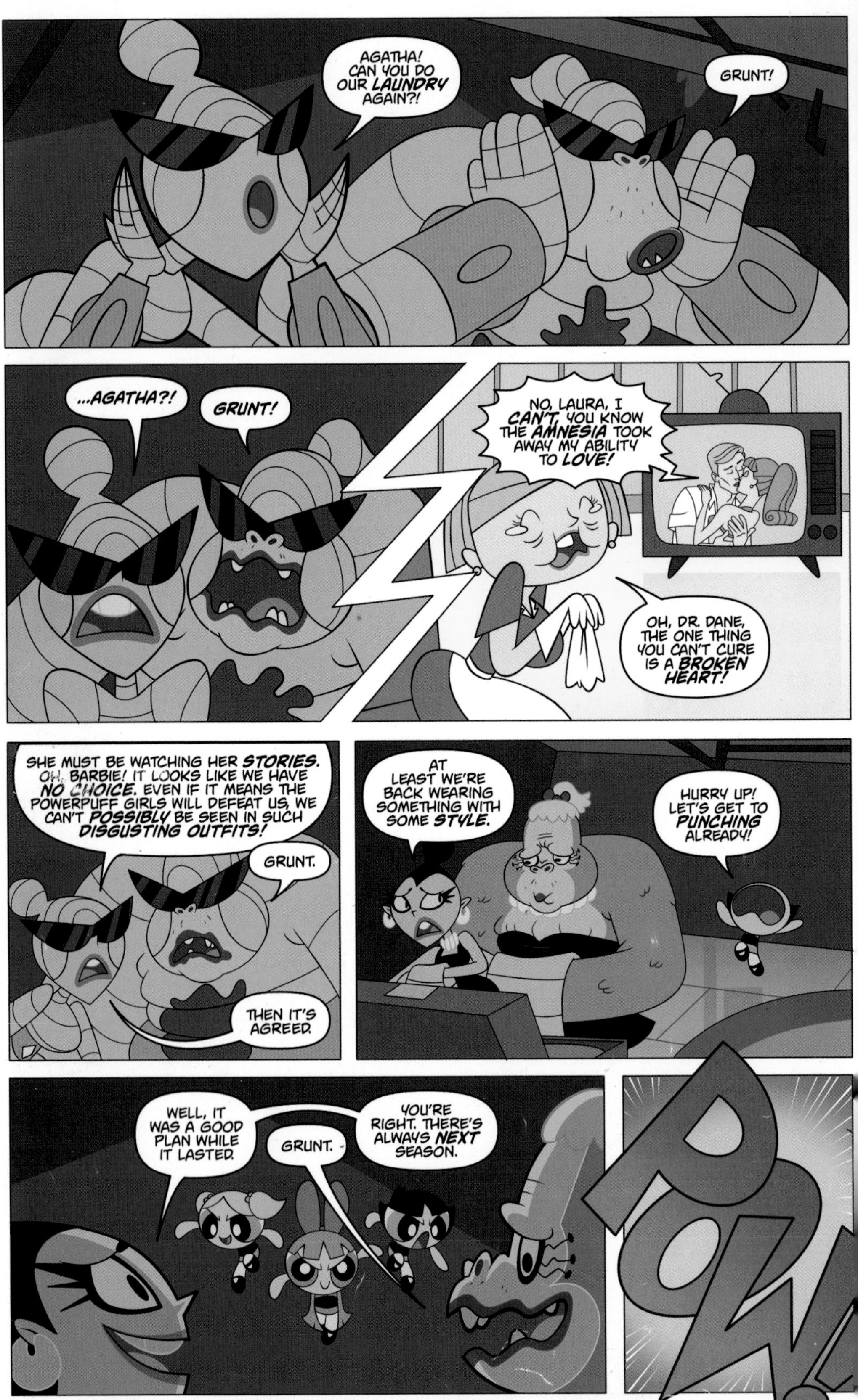
AGATHA! CAN YOU DO OUR LAUNDRY AGAIN?!
GRUNT!
...AGATHA?!
GRUNT!
NO, LAURA, I CAN'T, YOU KNOW THE AMNESIA TOOK AWAY MY ABILITY TO LOVE!
OH, DR. DANE, THE ONE THING YOU CAN'T CURE IS A BROKEN HEART!
SHE MUST BE WATCHING HER STORIES. OH, BARBIE! IT LOOKS LIKE WE HAVE NO CHOICE. EVEN IF IT MEANS THE POWERPUFF GIRLS WILL DEFEAT US, WE CAN'T POSSIBLY BE SEEN IN SUCH DISGUSTING OUTFITS!
GRUNT.
THEN IT'S AGREED.
AT LEAST WE'RE BACK WEARING SOMETHING WITH SOME STYLE.
HURRY UP! LET'S GET TO PUNCHING ALREADY!
WELL, IT WAS A GOOD PLAN WHILE IT LASTED.
GRUNT.
YOU'RE RIGHT. THERE'S ALWAYS NEXT SEASON.
POW!

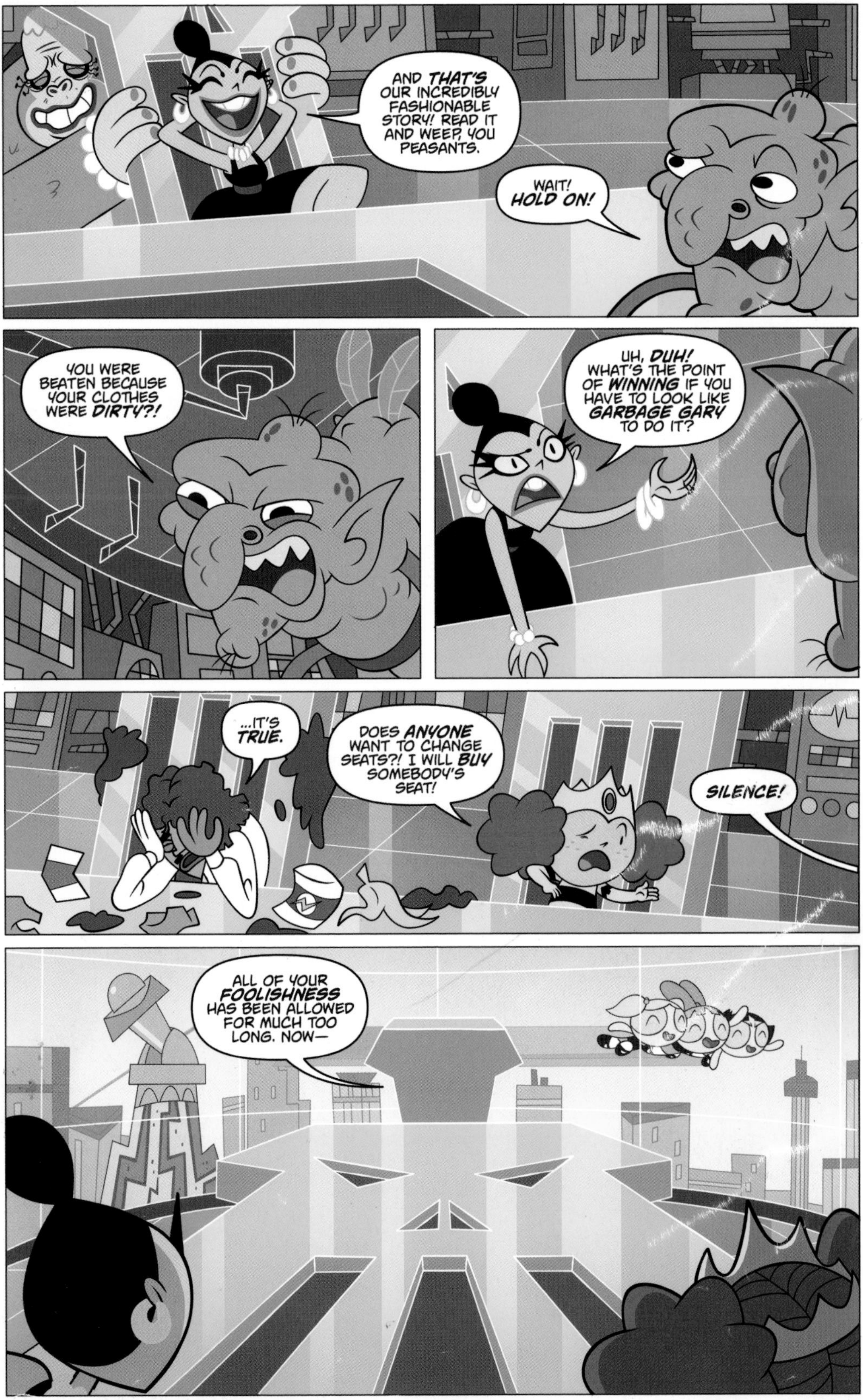
AND THAT'S OUR INCREDIBLY FASHIONABLE STORY! READ IT AND WEEP, YOU PEASANTS.
WAIT! HOLD ON!
YOU WERE BEATEN BECAUSE YOUR CLOTHES WERE DIRTY?!
UH, DUH! WHAT'S THE POINT OF WINNING IF YOU HAVE TO LOOK LIKE GARBAGE GARY TO DO IT?
...IT'S TRUE.
DOES ANYONE WANT TO CHANGE SEATS?! I WILL BUY SOMEBODY'S SEAT!
SILENCE!
ALL OF YOUR FOOLISHNESS HAS BEEN ALLOWED FOR MUCH TOO LONG. NOW—

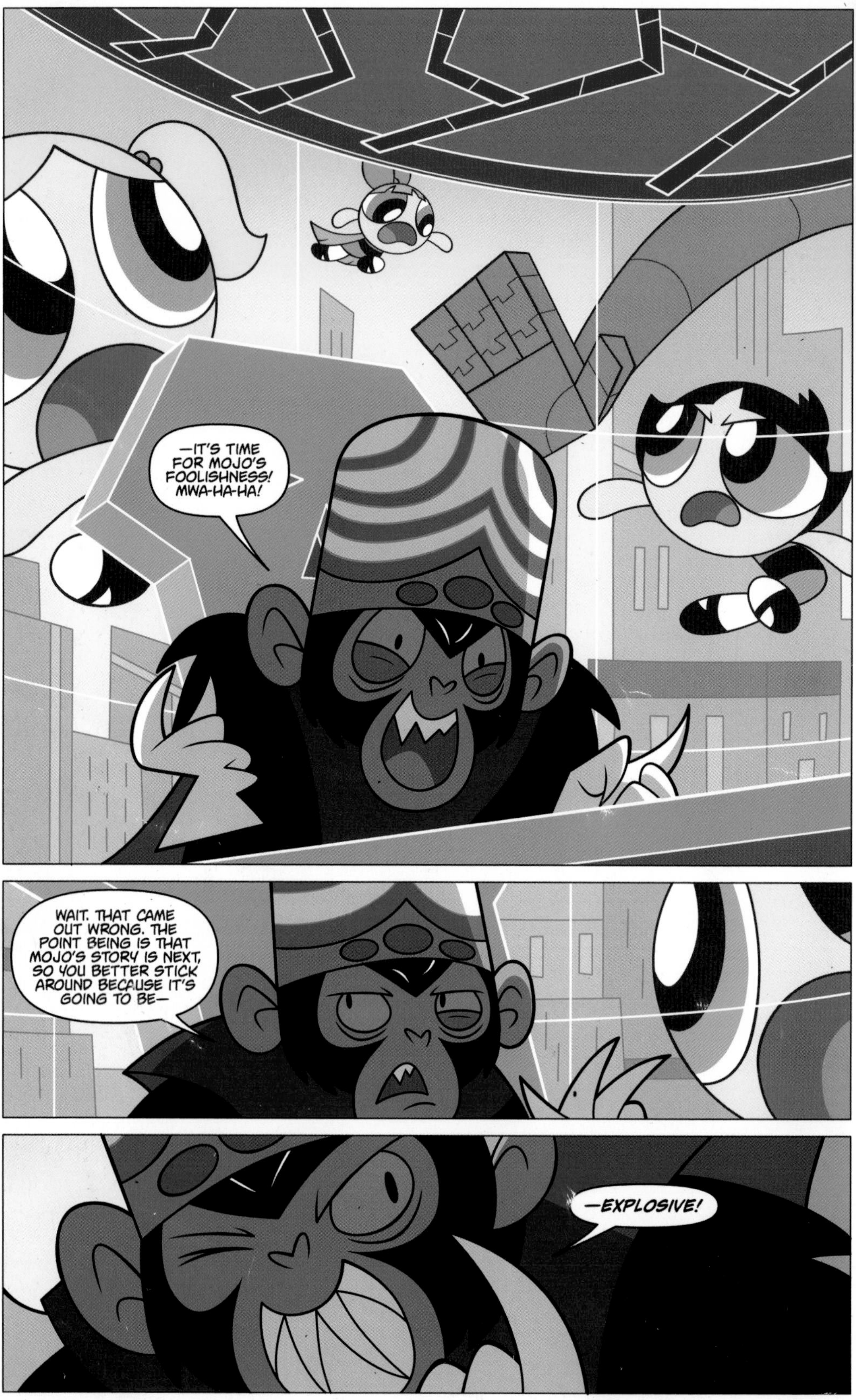
—IT'S TIME FOR MOJO'S FOOLISHNESS! MWA-HA-HA!
WAIT. THAT CAME OUT WRONG. THE POINT BEING IS THAT MOJO'S STORY IS NEXT, SO YOU BETTER STICK AROUND BECAUSE IT'S GOING TO BE—
—EXPLOSIVE!

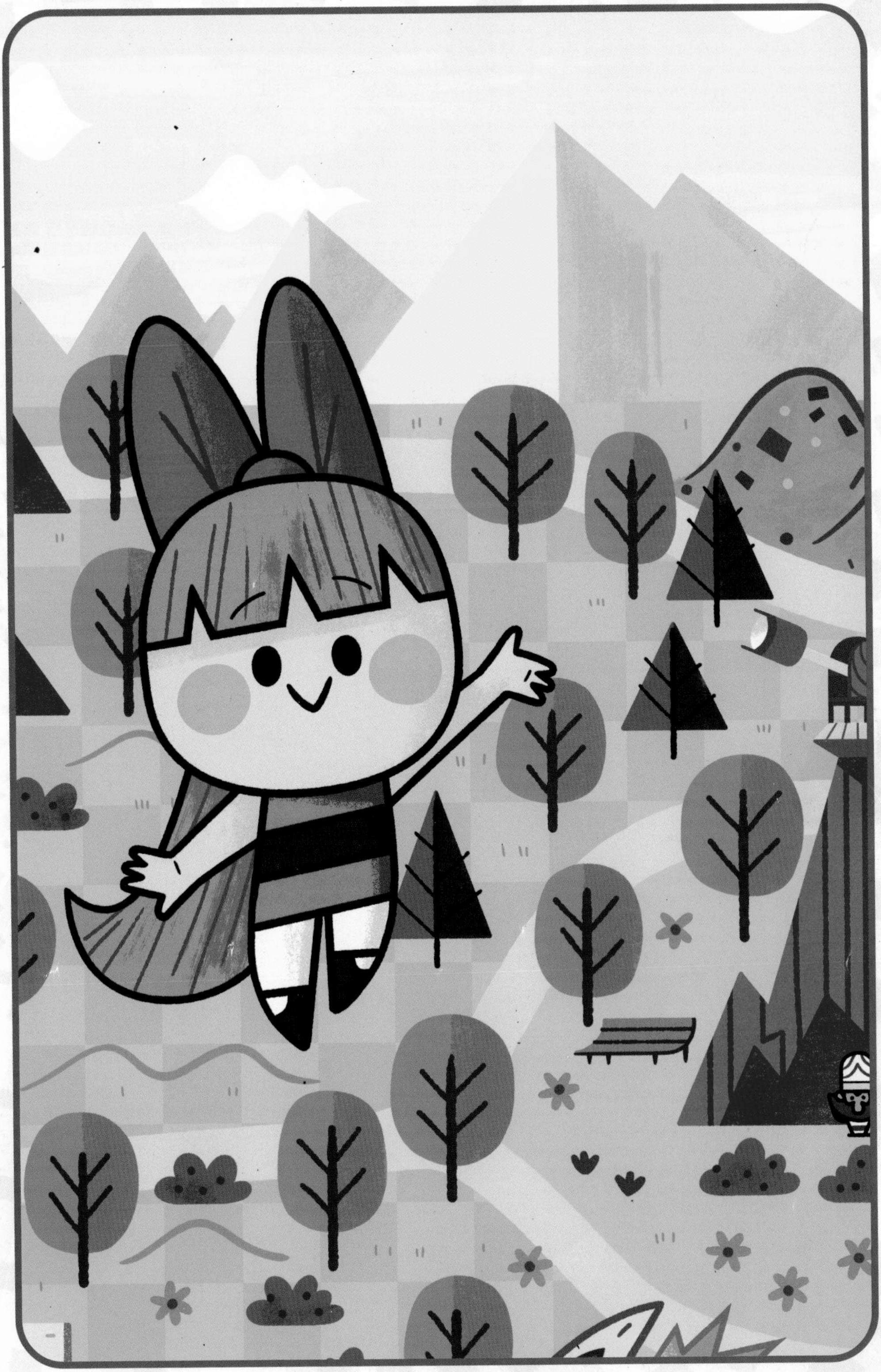

Cover Art by **Andrew Kolb**

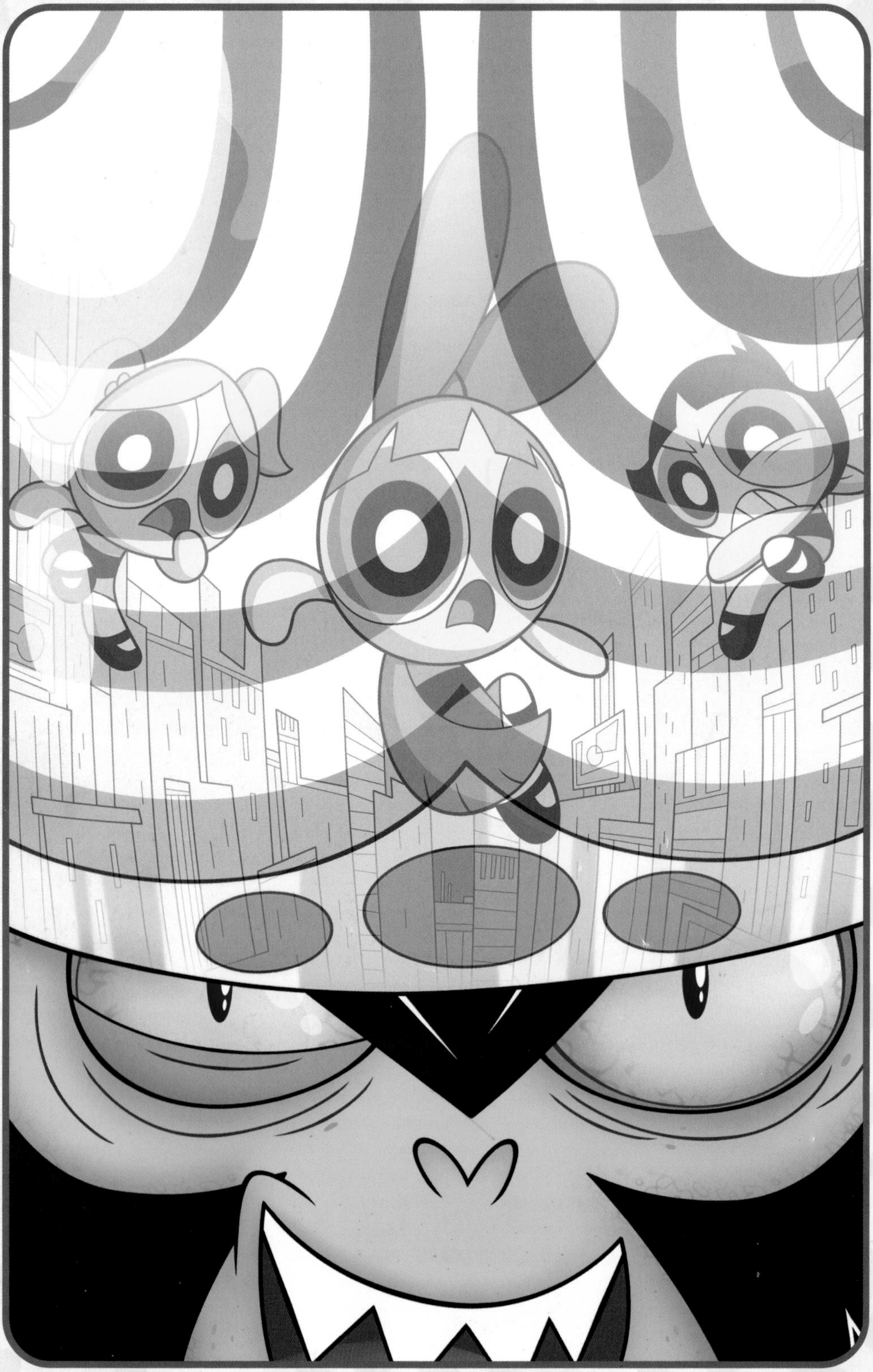

Cover Art by **Philip Murphy**

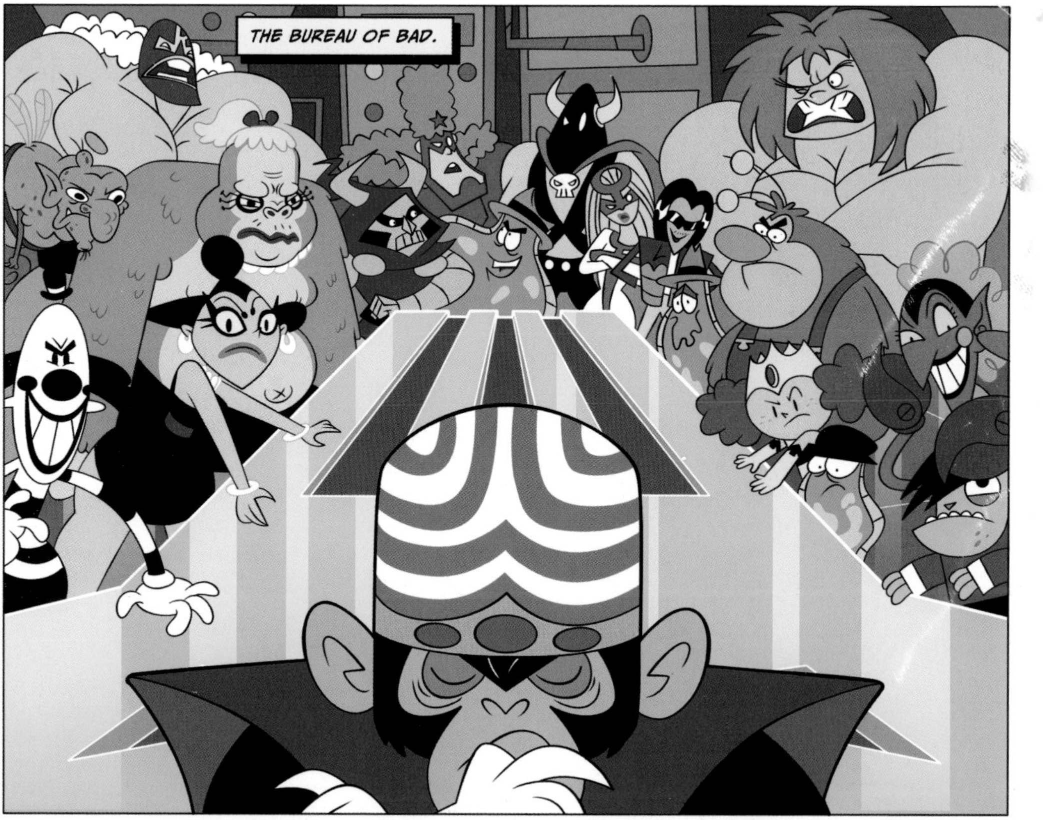
THE BUREAU OF BAD.

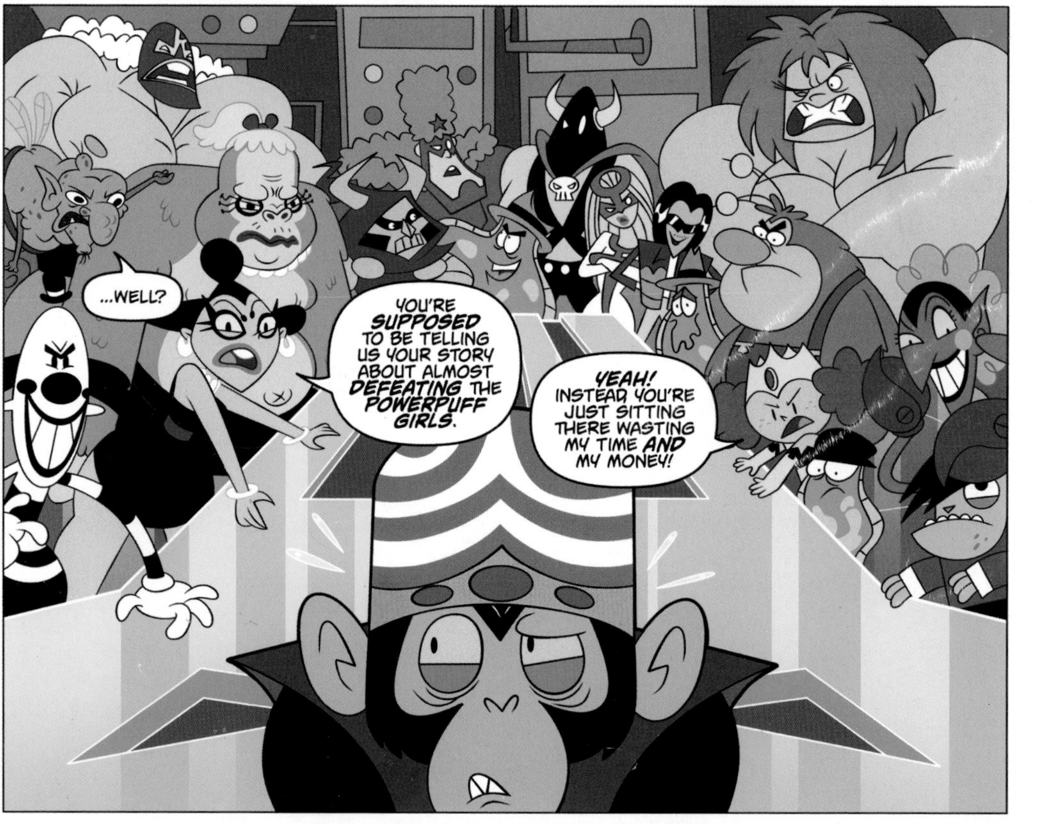
...WELL?
YOU'RE SUPPOSED TO BE TELLING US YOUR STORY ABOUT ALMOST DEFEATING THE POWERPUFF GIRLS.
YEAH! INSTEAD YOU'RE JUST SITTING THERE WASTING MY TIME AND MY MONEY!

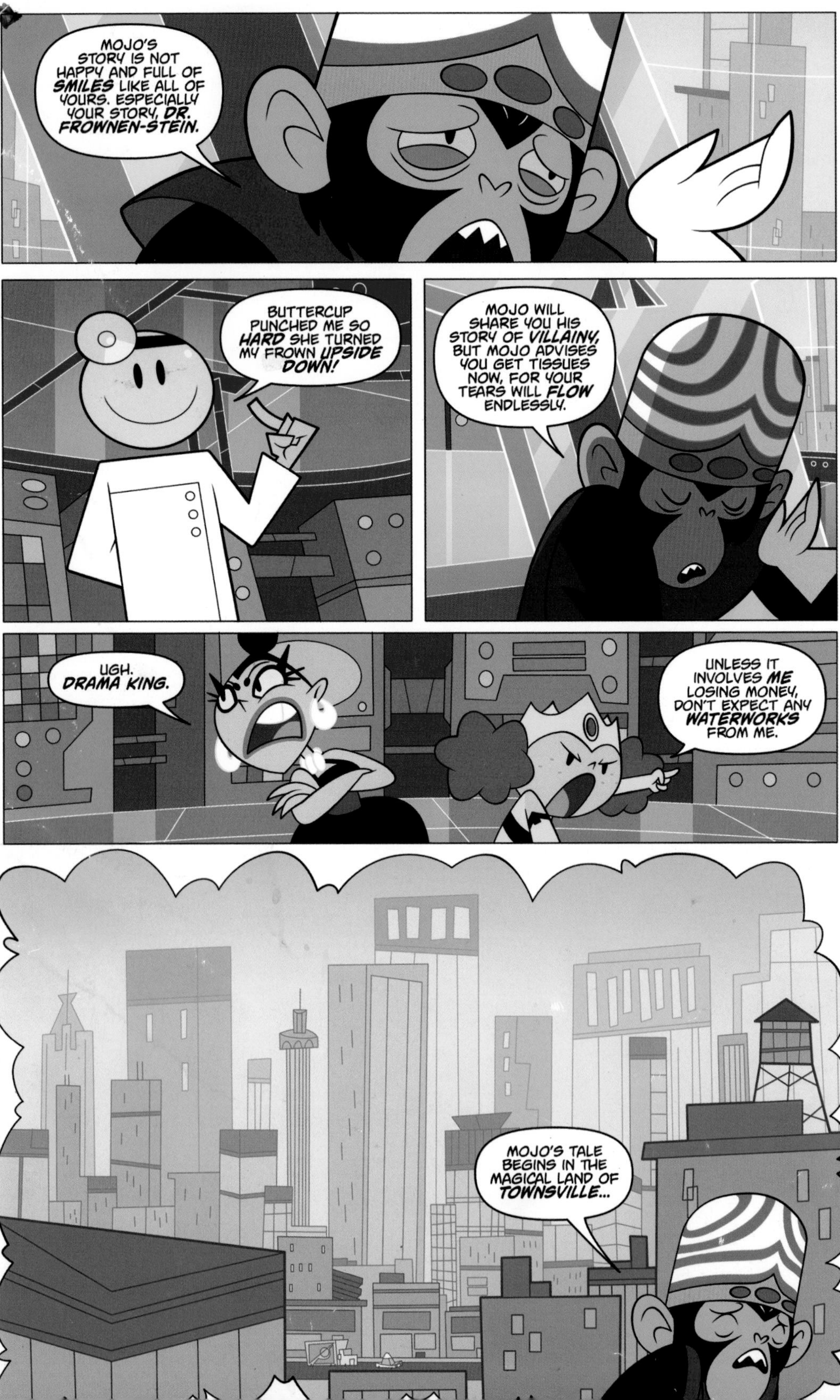
MOJO'S STORY IS NOT HAPPY AND FULL OF SMILES LIKE ALL OF YOURS. ESPECIALLY YOUR STORY, DR. FROWNEN-STEIN.
BUTTERCUP PUNCHED ME SO HARD SHE TURNED MY FROWN UPSIDE DOWN!
MOJO WILL SHARE YOU HIS STORY OF VILLAINY, BUT MOJO ADVISES YOU GET TISSUES NOW, FOR YOUR TEARS WILL FLOW ENDLESSLY.
UGH. DRAMA KING.
UNLESS IT INVOLVES ME LOSING MONEY, DON'T EXPECT ANY WATERWORKS FROM ME.
MOJO'S TALE BEGINS IN THE MAGICAL LAND OF TOWNSVILLE...

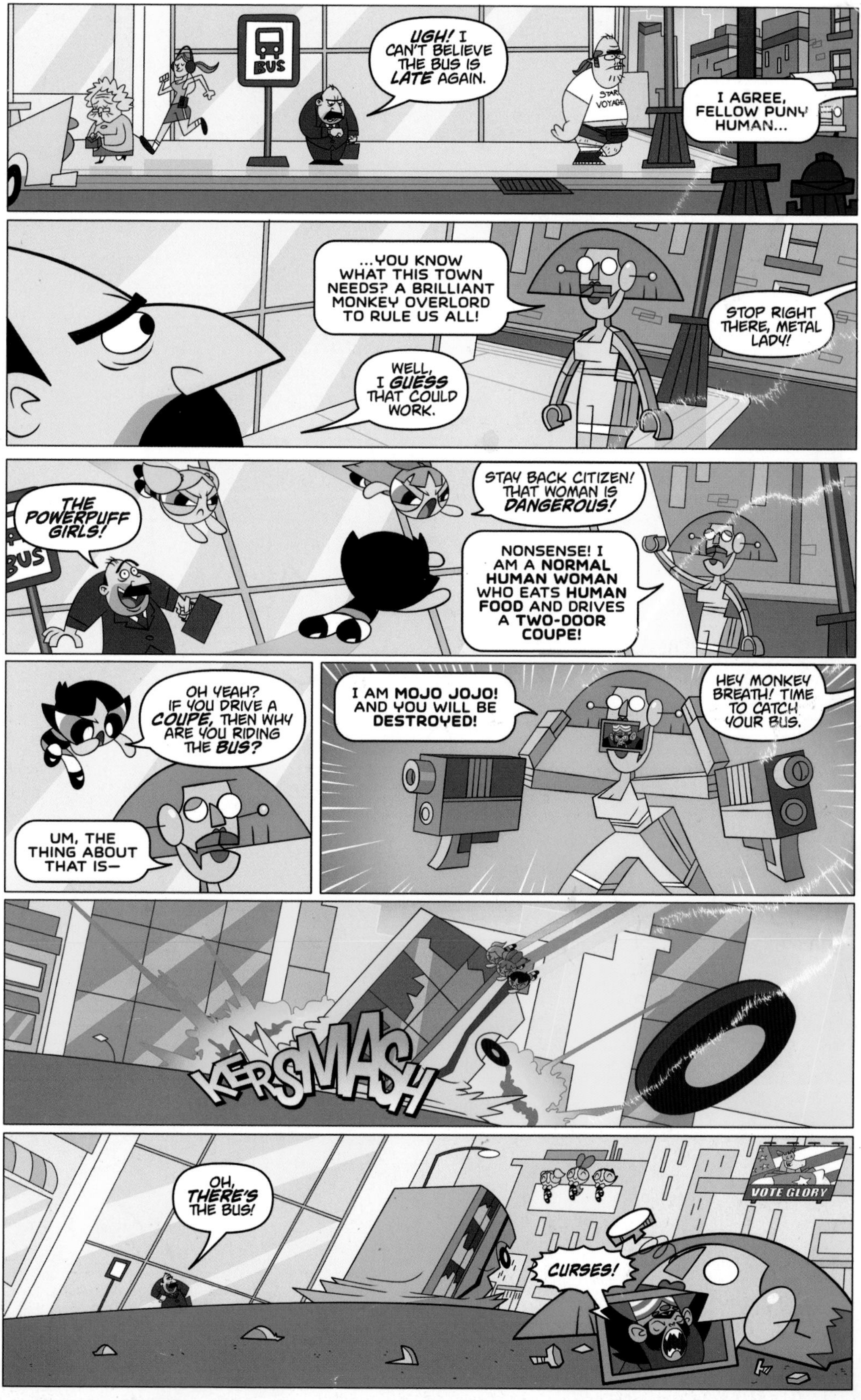
BUS
UGH! I CAN'T BELIEVE THE BUS IS LATE AGAIN.
STAR VOYAGE
I AGREE, FELLOW PUNY HUMAN...
...YOU KNOW WHAT THIS TOWN NEEDS? A BRILLIANT MONKEY OVERLORD TO RULE US ALL!
WELL, I GUESS THAT COULD WORK.
STOP RIGHT THERE, METAL LADY!
THE POWERPUFF GIRLS!
STAY BACK CITIZEN! THAT WOMAN IS DANGEROUS!
NONSENSE! I AM A NORMAL HUMAN WOMAN WHO EATS HUMAN FOOD AND DRIVES A TWO-DOOR COUPE!
OH YEAH? IF YOU DRIVE A COUPE, THEN WHY ARE YOU RIDING THE BUS?
UM, THE THING ABOUT THAT IS—
I AM MOJO JOJO! AND YOU WILL BE DESTROYED!
HEY MONKEY BREATH! TIME TO CATCH YOUR BUS.
KERSMASH
OH, THERE'S THE BUS!
VOTE GLORY
CURSES!

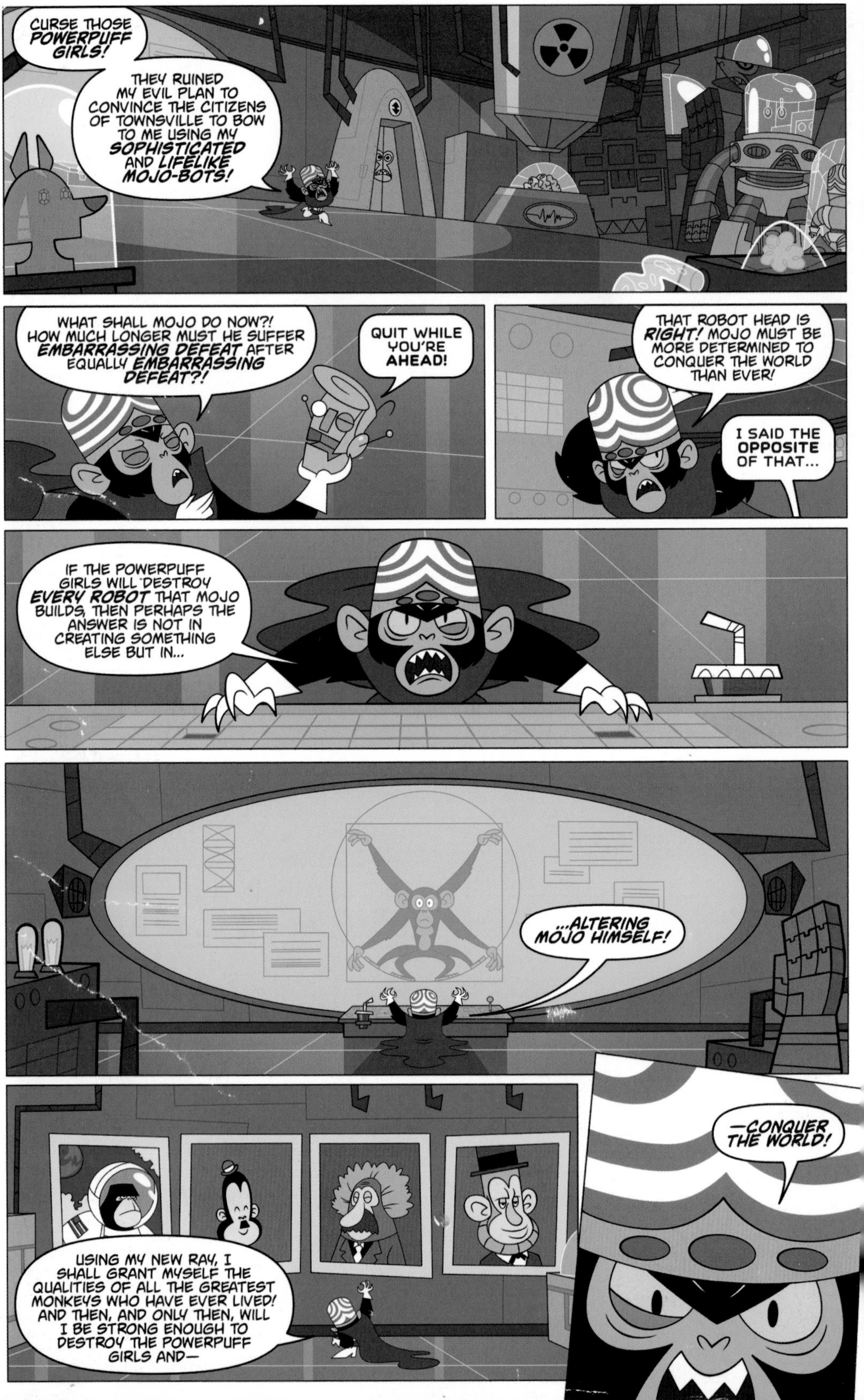
CURSE THOSE POWERPUFF GIRLS!
THEY RUINED MY EVIL PLAN TO CONVINCE THE CITIZENS OF TOWNSVILLE TO BOW TO ME USING MY SOPHISTICATED AND LIFELIKE MOJO-BOTS!
WHAT SHALL MOJO DO NOW?! HOW MUCH LONGER MUST HE SUFFER EMBARRASSING DEFEAT AFTER EQUALLY EMBARRASSING DEFEAT?!
QUIT WHILE YOU'RE AHEAD!
THAT ROBOT HEAD IS RIGHT! MOJO MUST BE MORE DETERMINED TO CONQUER THE WORLD THAN EVER!
I SAID THE OPPOSITE OF THAT...
IF THE POWERPUFF GIRLS WILL DESTROY EVERY ROBOT THAT MOJO BUILDS, THEN PERHAPS THE ANSWER IS NOT IN CREATING SOMETHING ELSE BUT IN...
...ALTERING MOJO HIMSELF!
USING MY NEW RAY, I SHALL GRANT MYSELF THE QUALITIES OF ALL THE GREATEST MONKEYS WHO HAVE EVER LIVED! AND THEN, AND ONLY THEN, WILL I BE STRONG ENOUGH TO DESTROY THE POWERPUFF GIRLS AND—
—CONQUER THE WORLD!

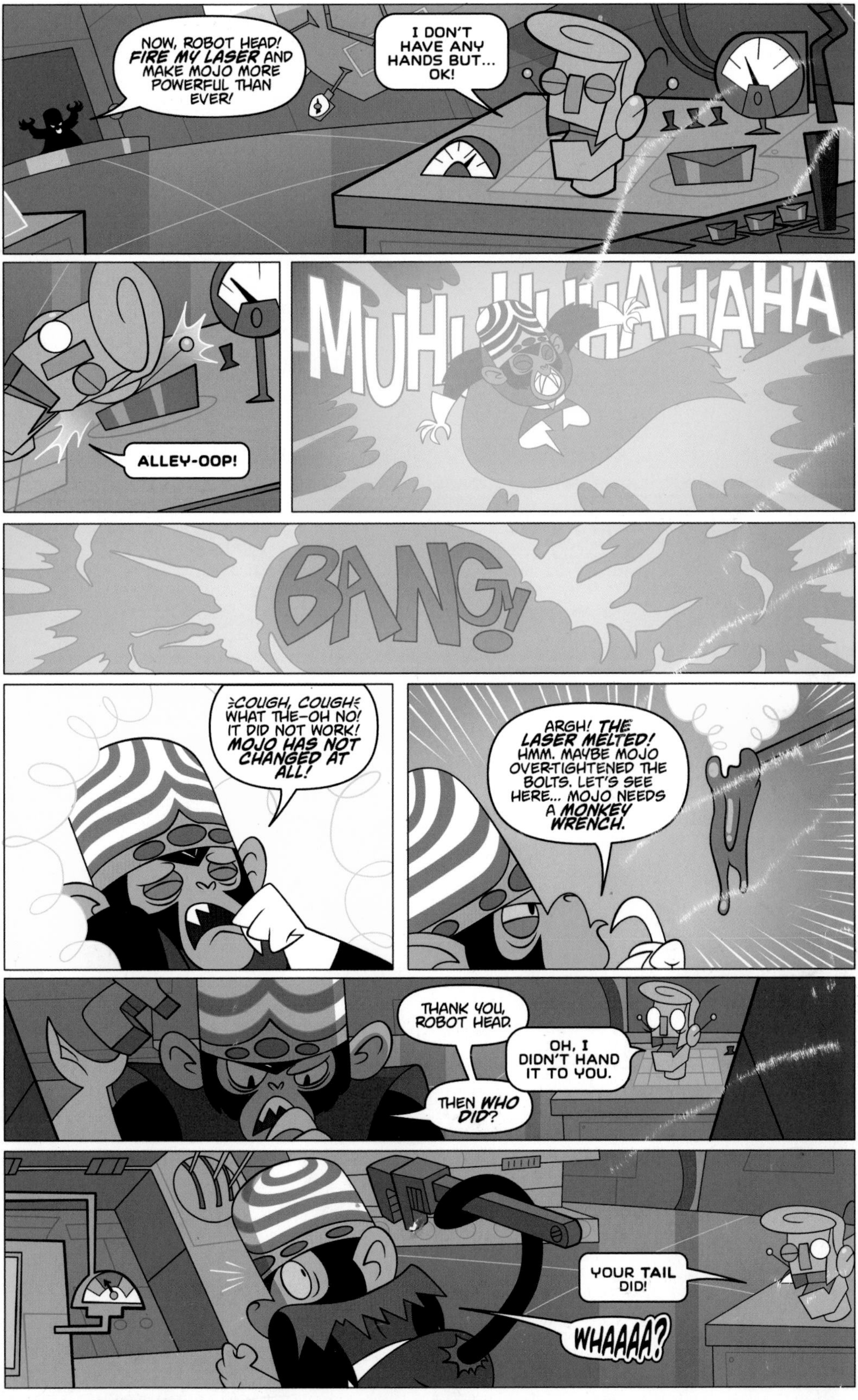
NOW, ROBOT HEAD! FIRE MY LASER AND MAKE MOJO MORE POWERFUL THAN EVER!
I DON'T HAVE ANY HANDS BUT... OK!
ALLEY-OOP!
MUHAHAHA
BANG!
COUGH, COUGH WHAT THE—OH NO! IT DID NOT WORK! MOJO HAS NOT CHANGED AT ALL!
ARGH! THE LASER MELTED! HMM. MAYBE MOJO OVER-TIGHTENED THE BOLTS. LET'S SEE HERE... MOJO NEEDS A MONKEY WRENCH.
THANK YOU, ROBOT HEAD.
OH, I DIDN'T HAND IT TO YOU.
THEN WHO DID?
YOUR TAIL DID!
WHAAAA?

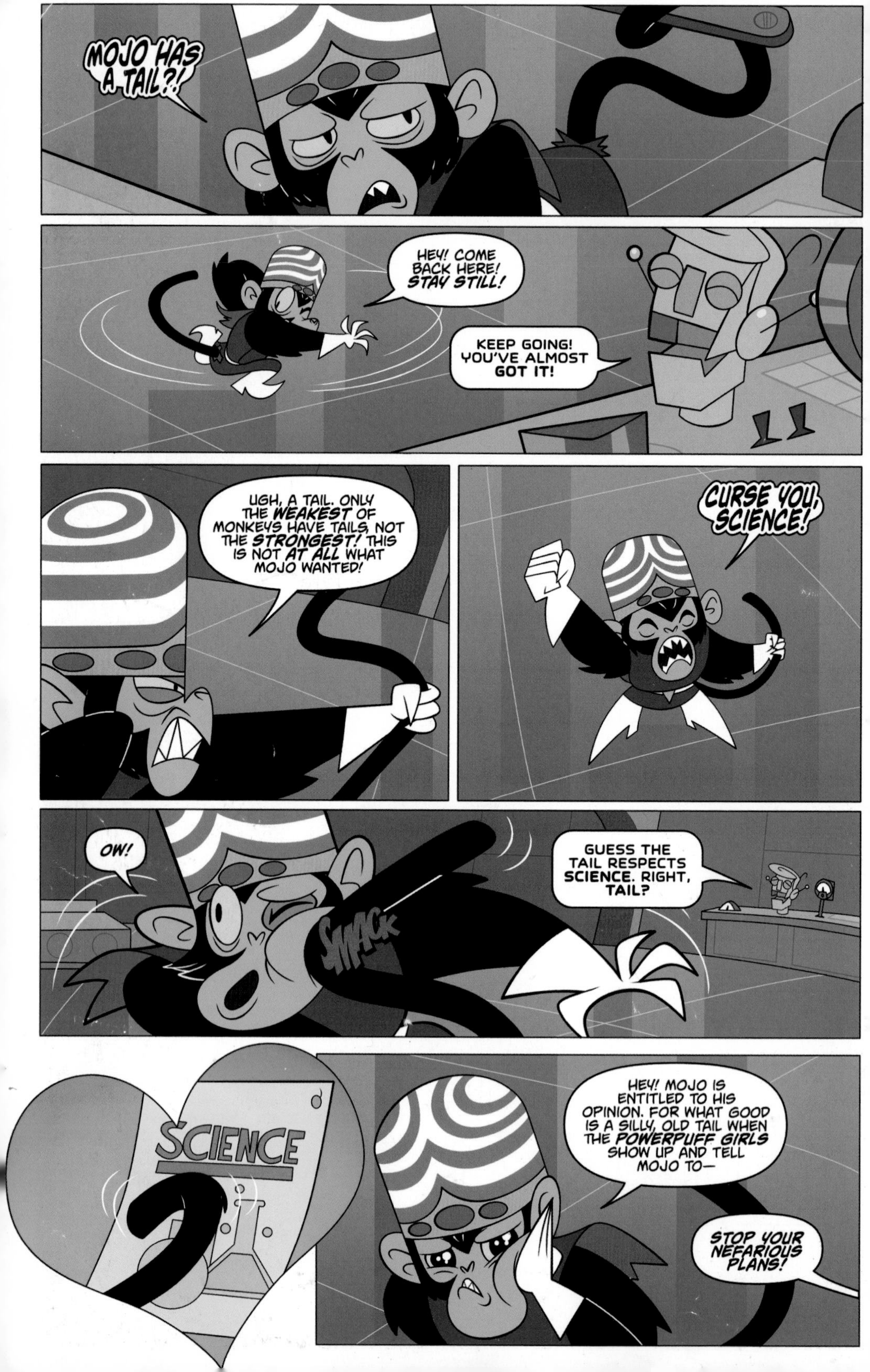
MOJO HAS A TAIL?!
HEY! COME BACK HERE! STAY STILL!
KEEP GOING! YOU'VE ALMOST GOT IT!
UGH, A TAIL. ONLY THE WEAKEST OF MONKEYS HAVE TAILS, NOT THE STRONGEST! THIS IS NOT AT ALL WHAT MOJO WANTED!
CURSE YOU, SCIENCE!
OW!
SMACK
GUESS THE TAIL RESPECTS SCIENCE. RIGHT, TAIL?
SCIENCE
HEY! MOJO IS ENTITLED TO HIS OPINION. FOR WHAT GOOD IS A SILLY, OLD TAIL WHEN THE POWERPUFF GIRLS SHOW UP AND TELL MOJO TO—
STOP YOUR NEFARIOUS PLANS!

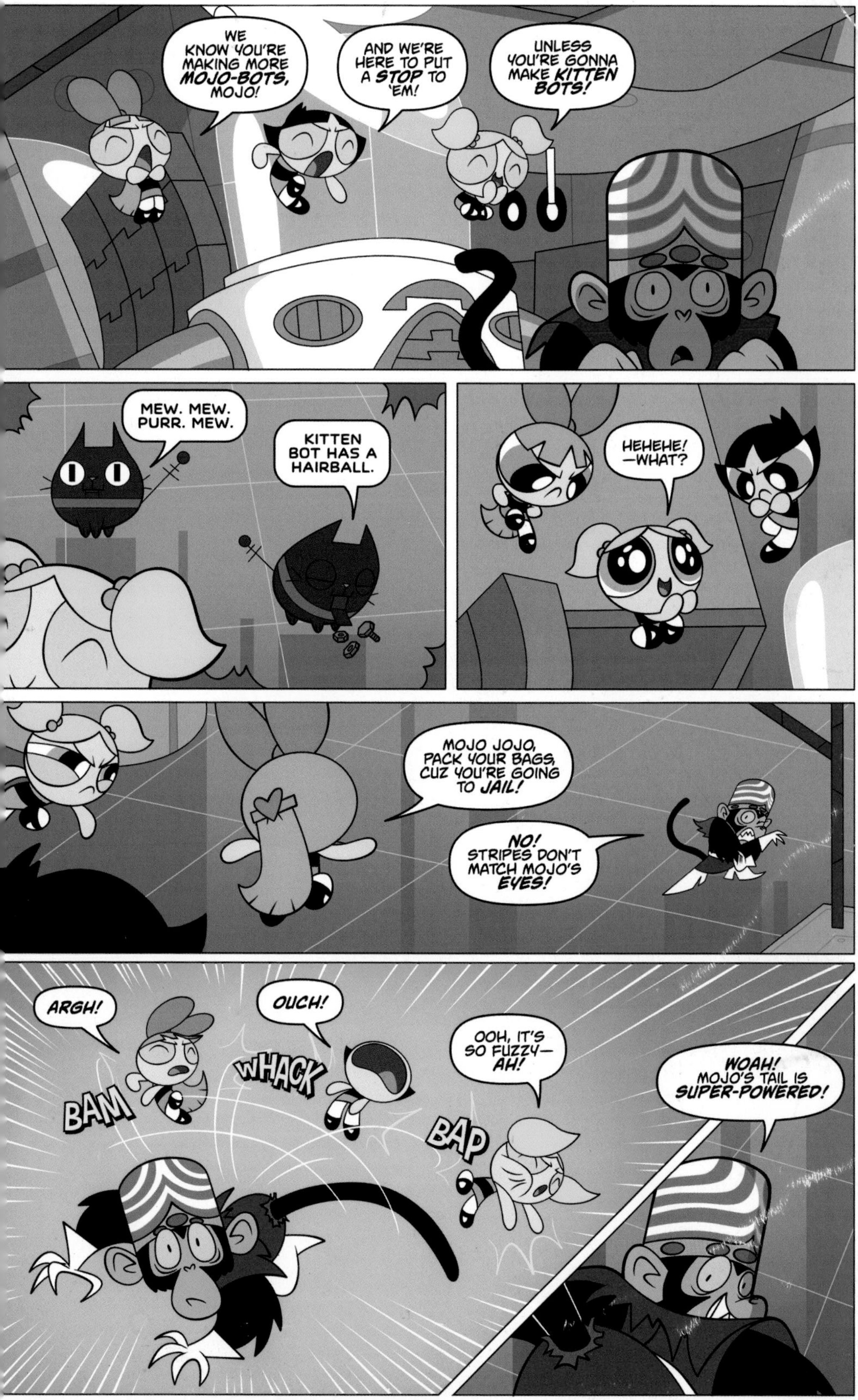

WE KNOW YOU'RE MAKING MORE MOJO-BOTS, MOJO!
AND WE'RE HERE TO PUT A STOP TO 'EM!
UNLESS YOU'RE GONNA MAKE KITTEN BOTS!
MEW. MEW. PURR. MEW.
KITTEN BOT HAS A HAIRBALL.
HEHEHE! —WHAT?
MOJO JOJO, PACK YOUR BAGS, CUZ YOU'RE GOING TO JAIL!
NO! STRIPES DON'T MATCH MOJO'S EYES!
ARGH!
BAM
WHACK
OUCH!
OOH, IT'S SO FUZZY— AH!
BAP
WOAH! MOJO'S TAIL IS SUPER-POWERED!

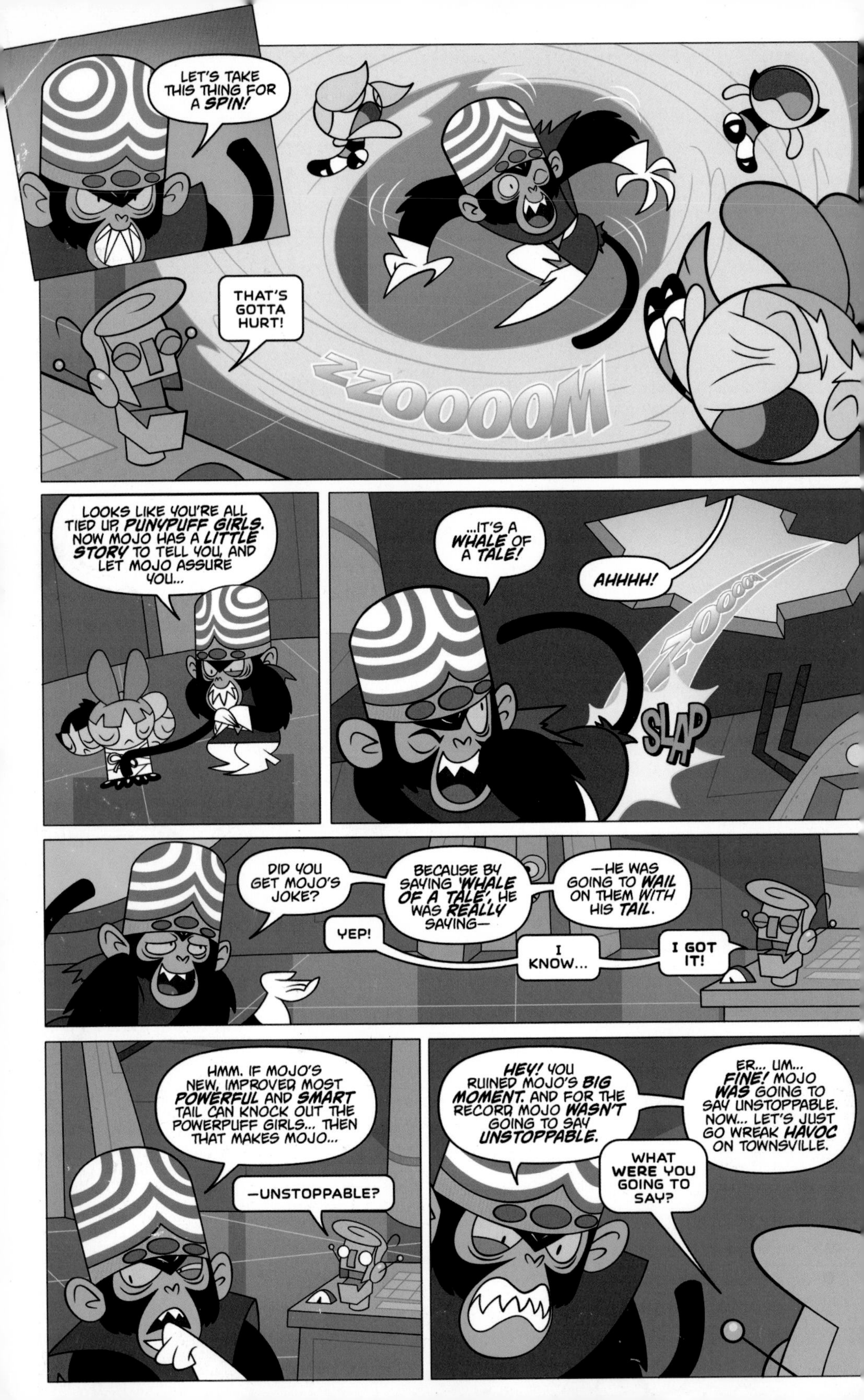

LET'S TAKE THIS THING FOR A SPIN!
THAT'S GOTTA HURT!
ZZOOOOOM
LOOKS LIKE YOU'RE ALL TIED UP, PUNYPUFF GIRLS. NOW MOJO HAS A LITTLE STORY TO TELL YOU, AND LET MOJO ASSURE YOU...
...IT'S A WHALE OF A TALE!
AHHHH!
ZOOOOM
SLAP
DID YOU GET MOJO'S JOKE?
BECAUSE BY SAYING 'WHALE OF A TALE', HE WAS REALLY SAYING—
—HE WAS GOING TO WAIL ON THEM WITH HIS TAIL.
YEP!
I KNOW...
I GOT IT!
HMM. IF MOJO'S NEW, IMPROVED MOST POWERFUL AND SMART TAIL CAN KNOCK OUT THE POWERPUFF GIRLS... THEN THAT MAKES MOJO...
—UNSTOPPABLE?
HEY! YOU RUINED MOJO'S BIG MOMENT. AND FOR THE RECORD MOJO WASN'T GOING TO SAY UNSTOPPABLE.
WHAT WERE YOU GOING TO SAY?
ER... UM... FINE! MOJO WAS GOING TO SAY UNSTOPPABLE. NOW... LET'S JUST GO WREAK HAVOC ON TOWNSVILLE.

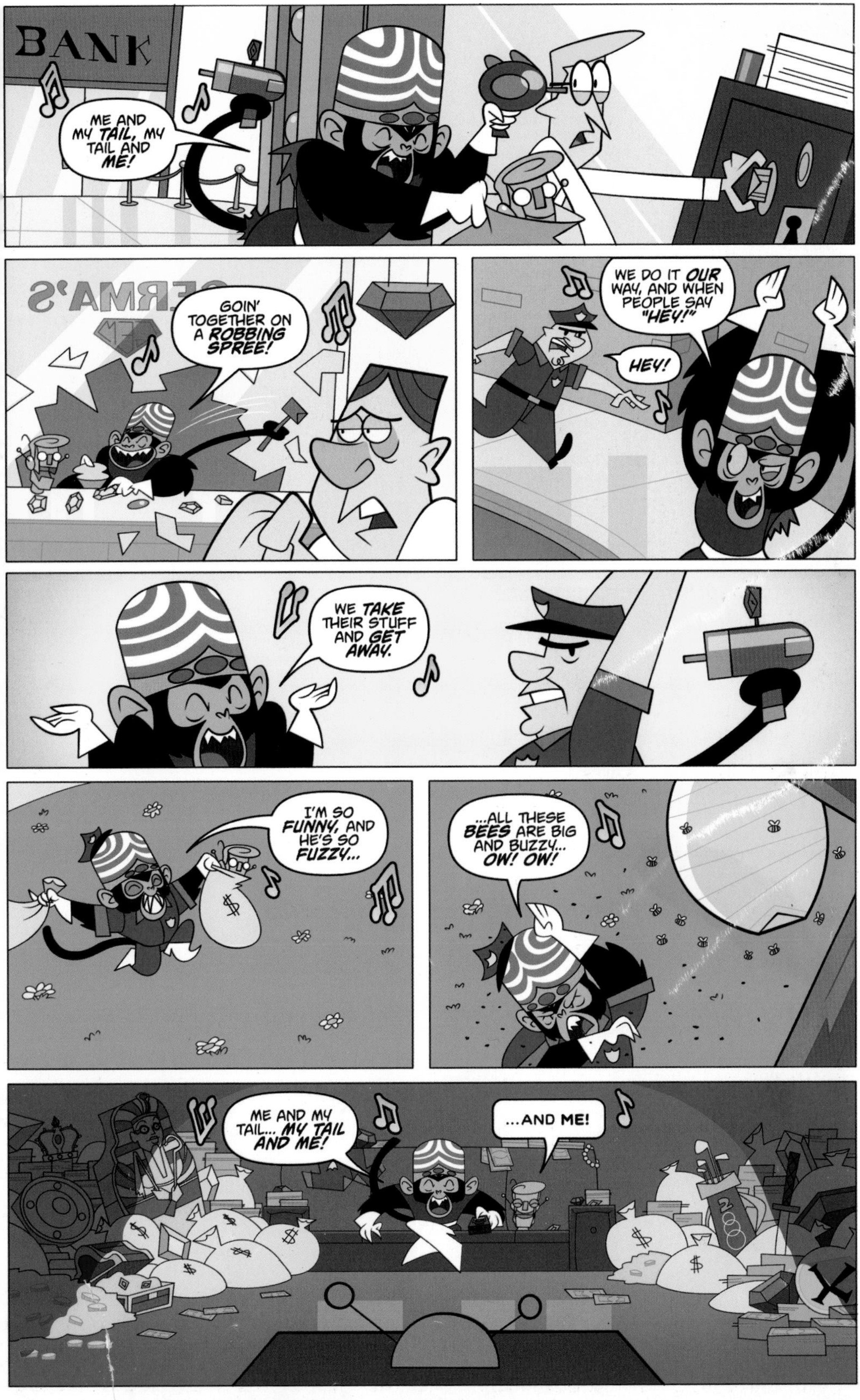
BANK
ME AND MY TAIL, MY TAIL AND ME!
ERMA'S
GOIN' TOGETHER ON A ROBBING SPREE!
WE DO IT OUR WAY, AND WHEN PEOPLE SAY "HEY!"
HEY!
WE TAKE THEIR STUFF AND GET AWAY.
I'M SO FUNNY, AND HE'S SO FUZZY...
...ALL THESE BEES ARE BIG AND BUZZY... OW! OW!
ME AND MY TAIL... MY TAIL AND ME!
...AND ME!

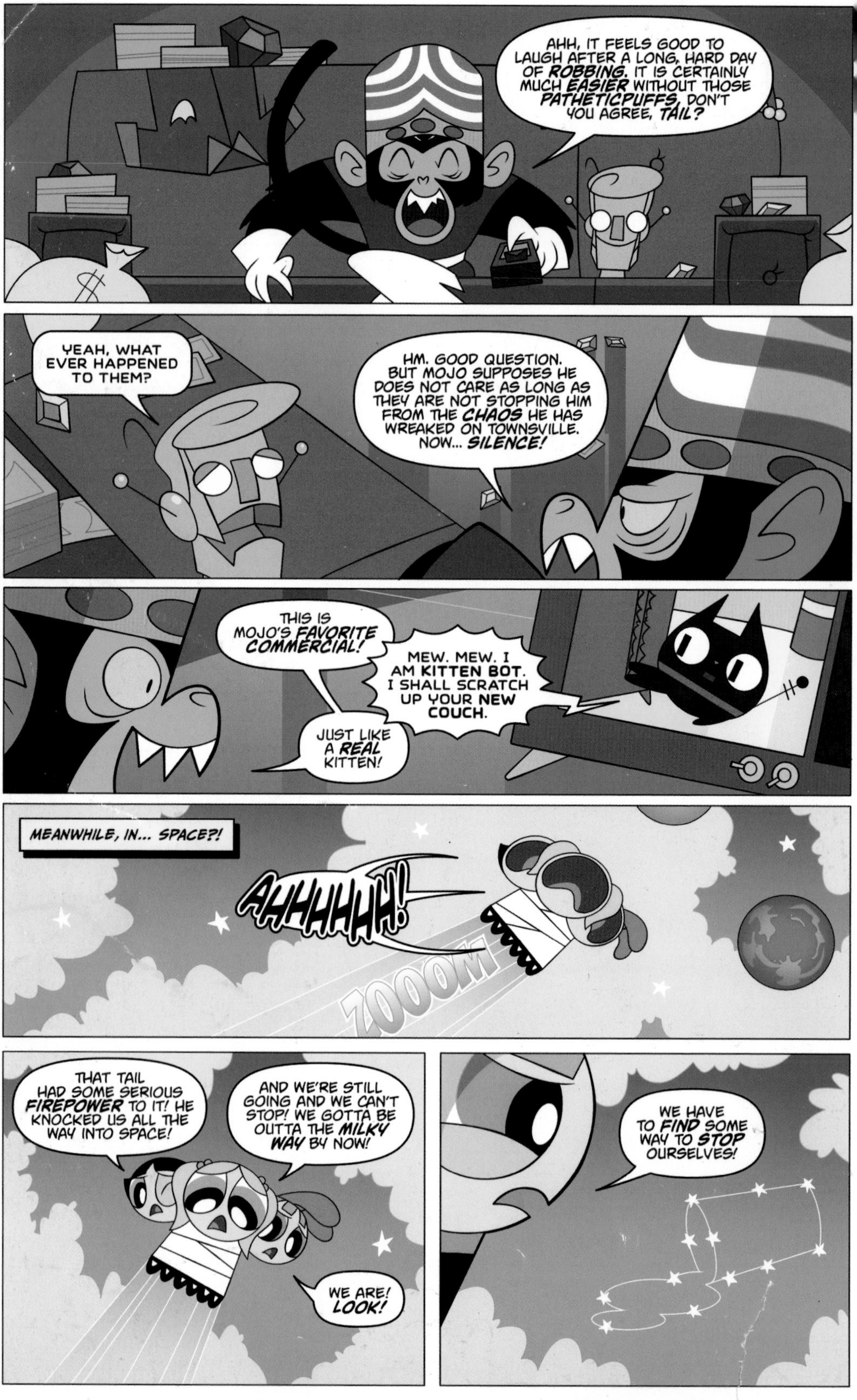
AHH, IT FEELS GOOD TO LAUGH AFTER A LONG, HARD DAY OF ROBBING. IT IS CERTAINLY MUCH EASIER WITHOUT THOSE PATHETICPUFFS, DON'T YOU AGREE, TAIL?
YEAH, WHAT EVER HAPPENED TO THEM?
HM. GOOD QUESTION. BUT MOJO SUPPOSES HE DOES NOT CARE AS LONG AS THEY ARE NOT STOPPING HIM FROM THE CHAOS HE HAS WREAKED ON TOWNSVILLE. NOW... SILENCE!
THIS IS MOJO'S FAVORITE COMMERCIAL!
MEW. MEW. I AM KITTEN BOT. I SHALL SCRATCH UP YOUR NEW COUCH.
JUST LIKE A REAL KITTEN!
MEANWHILE, IN... SPACE?!
AHHHHHH!
ZOOOM
THAT TAIL HAD SOME SERIOUS FIREPOWER TO IT! HE KNOCKED US ALL THE WAY INTO SPACE!
AND WE'RE STILL GOING AND WE CAN'T STOP! WE GOTTA BE OUTTA THE MILKY WAY BY NOW!
WE ARE! LOOK!
WE HAVE TO FIND SOME WAY TO STOP OURSELVES!

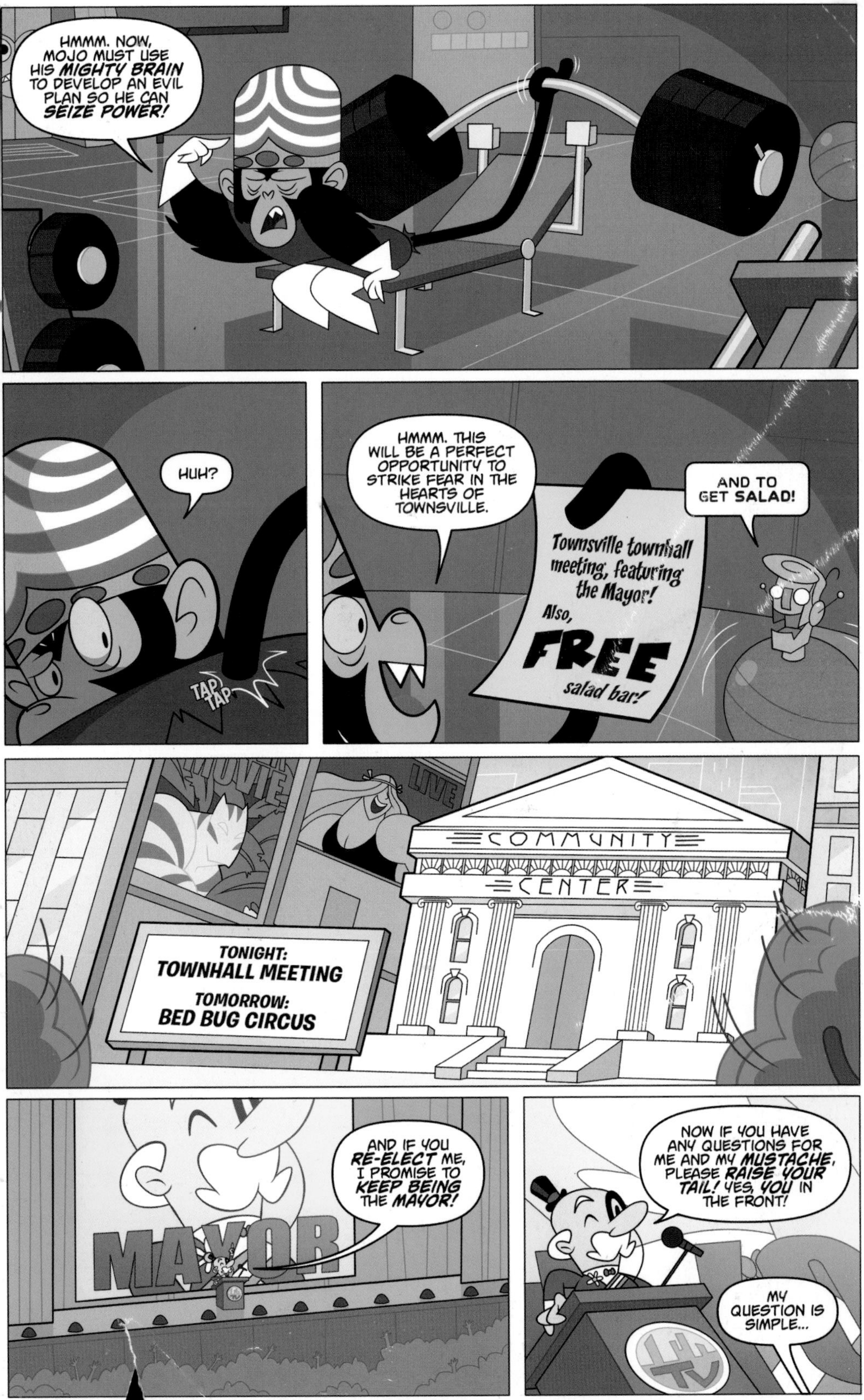
HMMM. NOW, MOJO MUST USE HIS MIGHTY BRAIN TO DEVELOP AN EVIL PLAN SO HE CAN SEIZE POWER!
HUH?
TAP TAP
HMMM. THIS WILL BE A PERFECT OPPORTUNITY TO STRIKE FEAR IN THE HEARTS OF TOWNSVILLE.
Townsville townhall meeting, featuring the Mayor! Also, FREE salad bar!
AND TO GET SALAD!
MOVIE
LIVE
COMMUNITY CENTER
TONIGHT: TOWNHALL MEETING
TOMORROW: BED BUG CIRCUS
AND IF YOU RE-ELECT ME, I PROMISE TO KEEP BEING THE MAYOR!
MAYOR
NOW IF YOU HAVE ANY QUESTIONS FOR ME AND MY MUSTACHE, PLEASE RAISE YOUR TAIL! YES, YOU IN THE FRONT!
MY QUESTION IS SIMPLE...

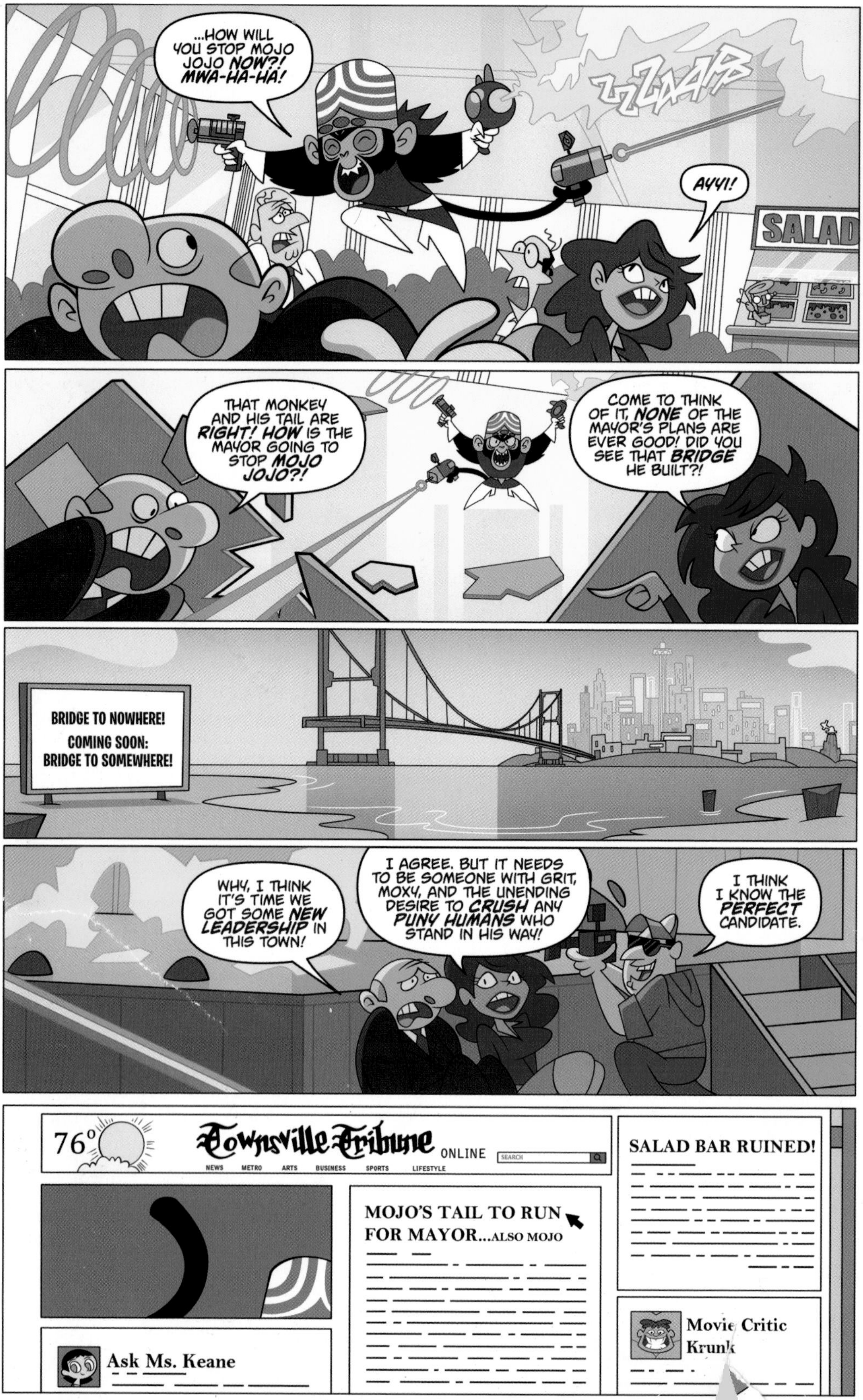
...HOW WILL YOU STOP MOJO JOJO NOW?! MWA-HA-HA!
ZZZAAPP
AYYI!
SALAD
THAT MONKEY AND HIS TAIL ARE RIGHT! HOW IS THE MAYOR GOING TO STOP MOJO JOJO?!
COME TO THINK OF IT, NONE OF THE MAYOR'S PLANS ARE EVER GOOD! DID YOU SEE THAT BRIDGE HE BUILT?!
BRIDGE TO NOWHERE!
COMING SOON: BRIDGE TO SOMEWHERE!
WHY, I THINK IT'S TIME WE GOT SOME NEW LEADERSHIP IN THIS TOWN!
I AGREE. BUT IT NEEDS TO BE SOMEONE WITH GRIT, MOXY, AND THE UNENDING DESIRE TO CRUSH ANY PUNY HUMANS WHO STAND IN HIS WAY!
I THINK I KNOW THE PERFECT CANDIDATE.
76°
Townsville Tribune ONLINE
SEARCH
NEWS METRO ARTS BUSINESS SPORTS LIFESTYLE
MOJO'S TAIL TO RUN FOR MAYOR...ALSO MOJO
SALAD BAR RUINED!
Ask Ms. Keane
Movie Critic Krunk

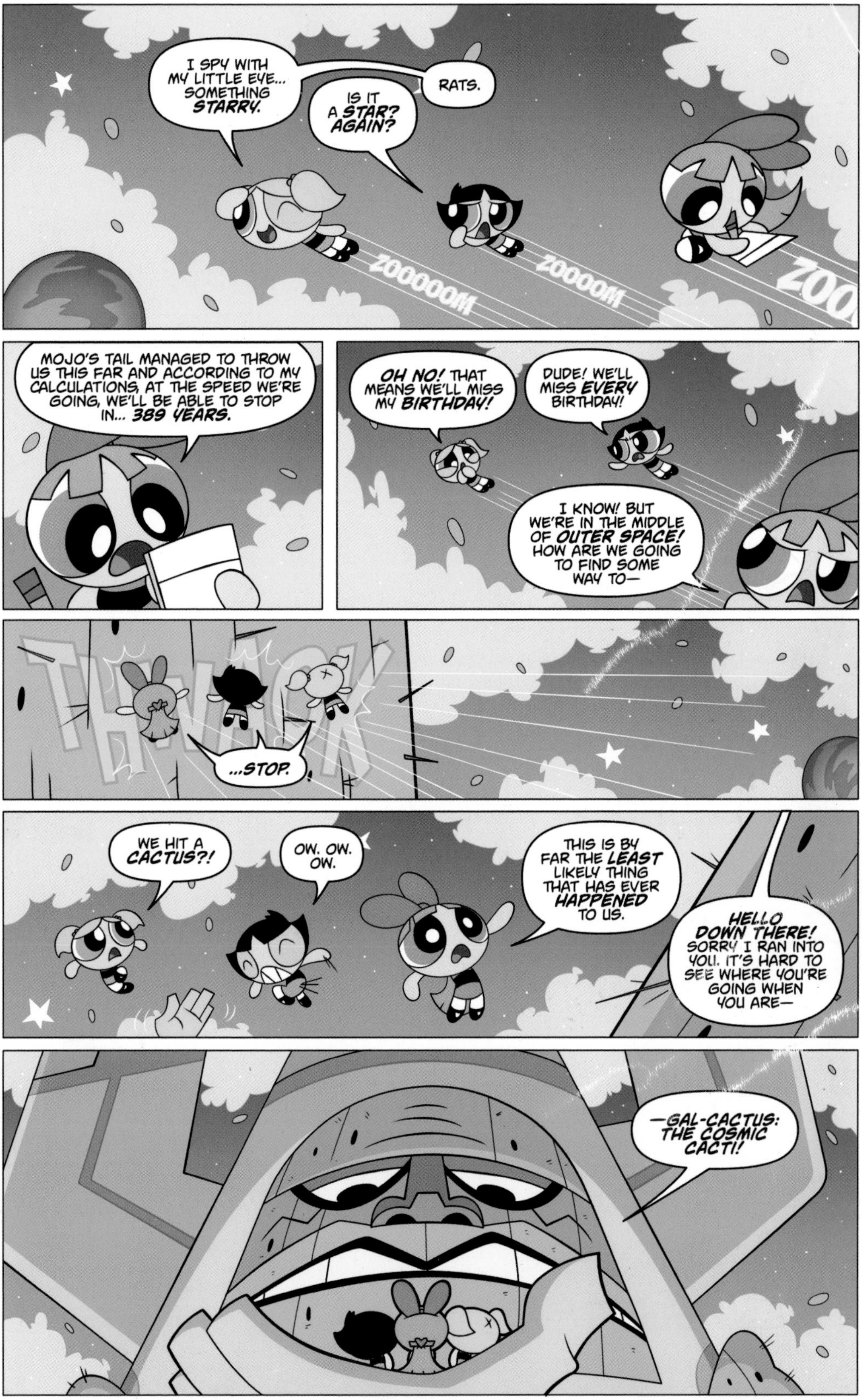
I SPY WITH MY LITTLE EYE... SOMETHING STARRY.
IS IT A STAR? AGAIN?
RATS.
ZOOOOOM
ZOOOOM
ZOO
MOJO'S TAIL MANAGED TO THROW US THIS FAR AND ACCORDING TO MY CALCULATIONS, AT THE SPEED WE'RE GOING, WE'LL BE ABLE TO STOP IN... 389 YEARS.
OH NO! THAT MEANS WE'LL MISS MY BIRTHDAY!
DUDE! WE'LL MISS EVERY BIRTHDAY!
I KNOW! BUT WE'RE IN THE MIDDLE OF OUTER SPACE! HOW ARE WE GOING TO FIND SOME WAY TO—
THWACK!
...STOP.
WE HIT A CACTUS?!
OW. OW. OW.
THIS IS BY FAR THE LEAST LIKELY THING THAT HAS EVER HAPPENED TO US.
HELLO DOWN THERE! SORRY I RAN INTO YOU. IT'S HARD TO SEE WHERE YOU'RE GOING WHEN YOU ARE—
—GAL-CACTUS: THE COSMIC CACTI!

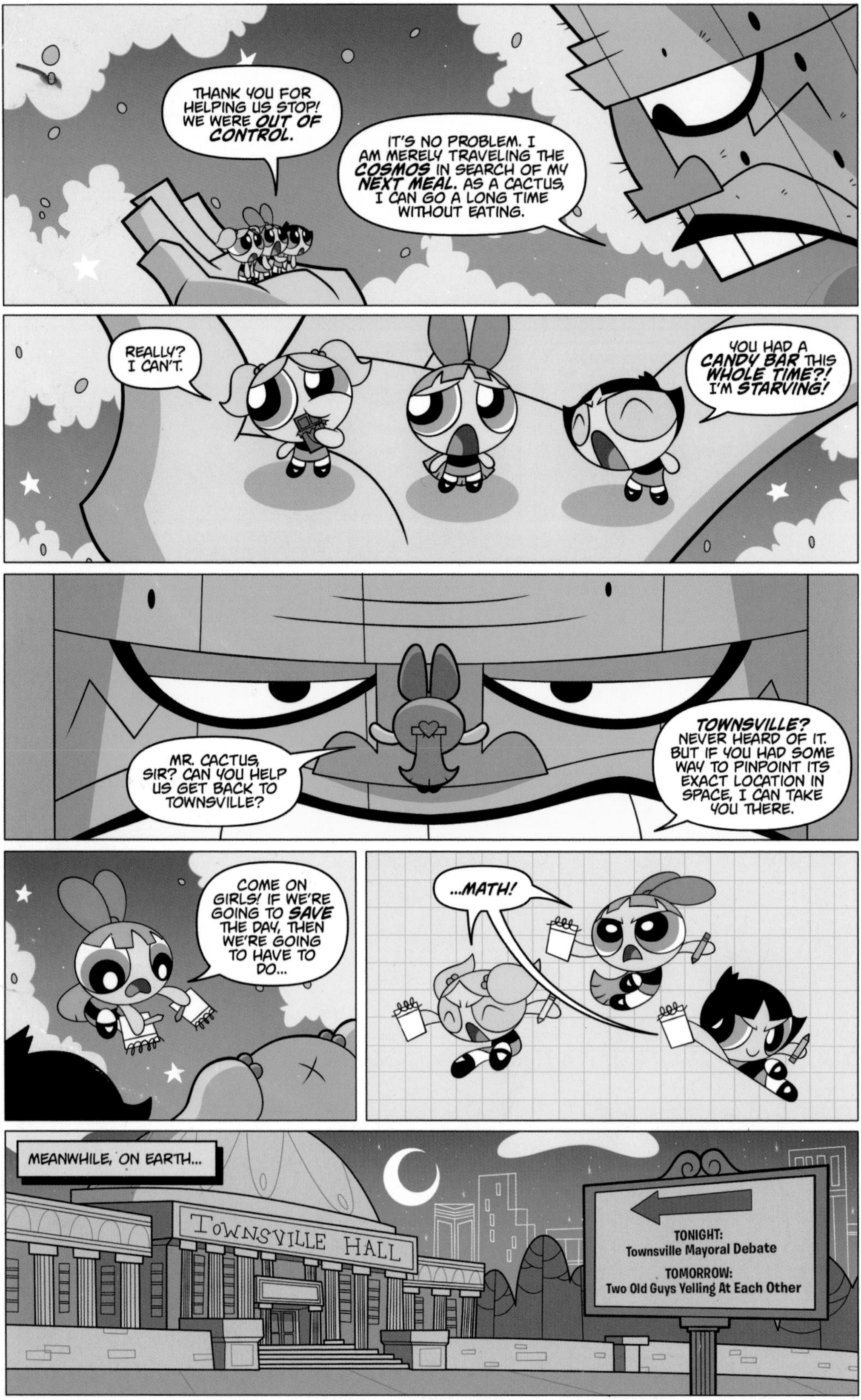
THANK YOU FOR HELPING US STOP! WE WERE OUT OF CONTROL.
IT'S NO PROBLEM. I AM MERELY TRAVELING THE COSMOS IN SEARCH OF MY NEXT MEAL. AS A CACTUS, I CAN GO A LONG TIME WITHOUT EATING.
REALLY? I CAN'T.
YOU HAD A CANDY BAR THIS WHOLE TIME?! I'M STARVING!
MR. CACTUS, SIR? CAN YOU HELP US GET BACK TO TOWNSVILLE?
TOWNSVILLE? NEVER HEARD OF IT. BUT IF YOU HAD SOME WAY TO PINPOINT ITS EXACT LOCATION IN SPACE, I CAN TAKE YOU THERE.
COME ON GIRLS! IF WE'RE GOING TO SAVE THE DAY, THEN WE'RE GOING TO HAVE TO DO...
...MATH!
MEANWHILE, ON EARTH...
TOWNSVILLE HALL
TONIGHT:
Townsville Mayoral Debate
TOMORROW:
Two Old Guys Yelling At Each Other

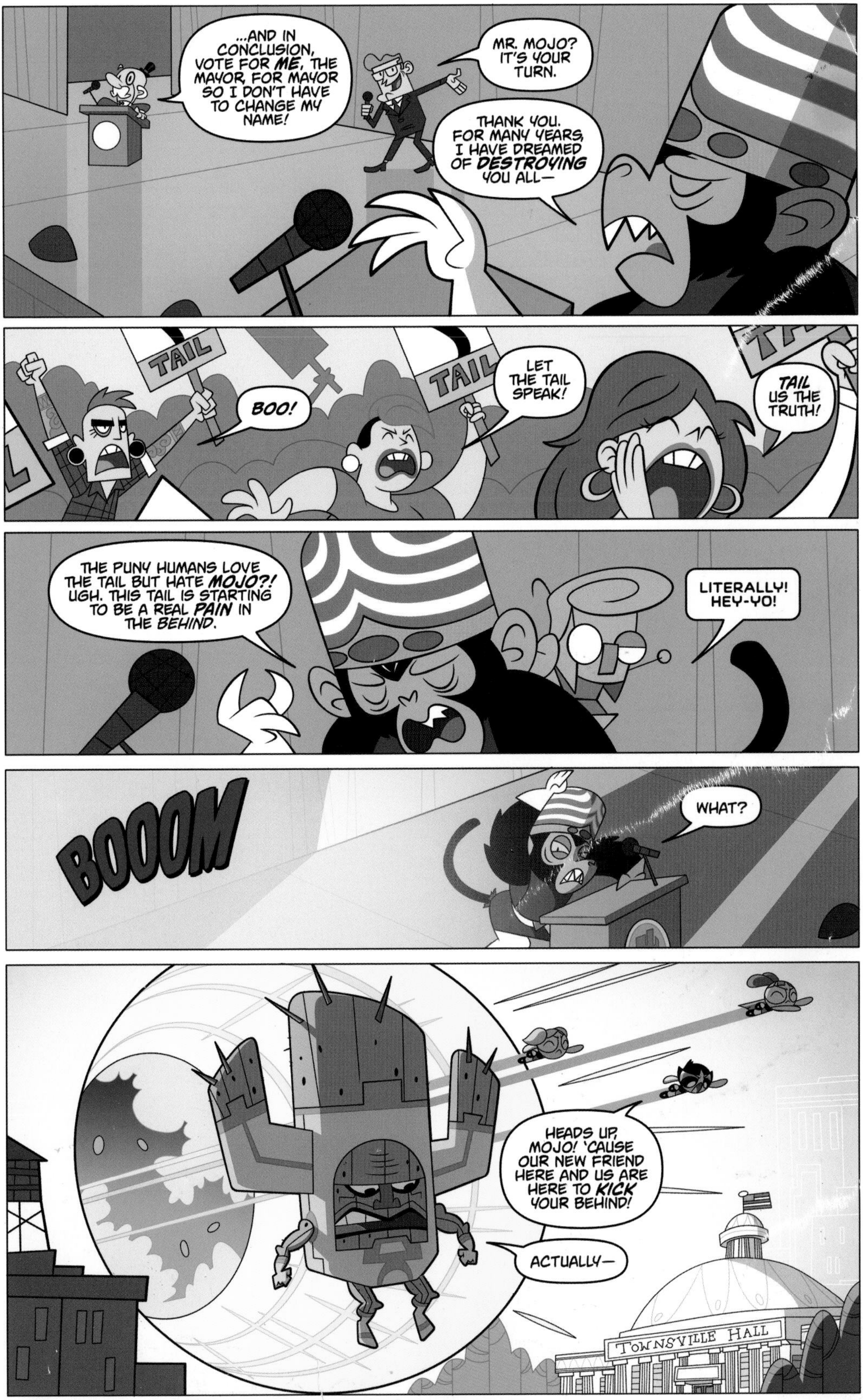
...AND IN CONCLUSION, VOTE FOR ME, THE MAYOR, FOR MAYOR SO I DON'T HAVE TO CHANGE MY NAME!
MR. MOJO? IT'S YOUR TURN.
THANK YOU. FOR MANY YEARS, I HAVE DREAMED OF DESTROYING YOU ALL—
TAIL
BOO!
TAIL
LET THE TAIL SPEAK!
TAIL US THE TRUTH!
THE PUNY HUMANS LOVE THE TAIL BUT HATE MOJO?! UGH. THIS TAIL IS STARTING TO BE A REAL PAIN IN THE BEHIND.
LITERALLY! HEY-YO!
BOOOM
WHAT?
HEADS UP, MOJO! 'CAUSE OUR NEW FRIEND HERE AND US ARE HERE TO KICK YOUR BEHIND!
ACTUALLY—
TOWNSVILLE HALL

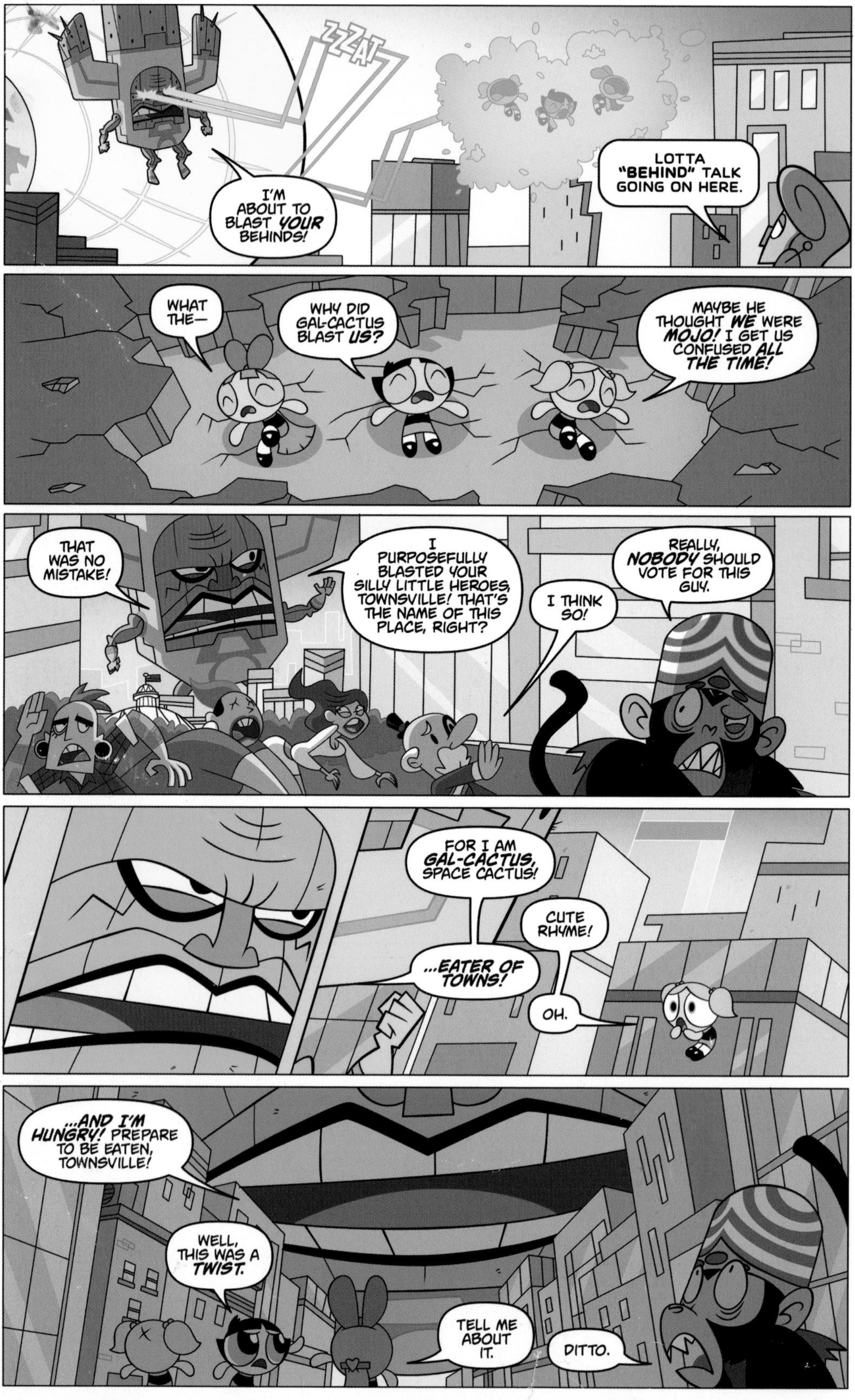
ZZZAT
I'M ABOUT TO BLAST YOUR BEHINDS!
LOTTA "BEHIND" TALK GOING ON HERE.
WHAT THE—
WHY DID GAL-CACTUS BLAST US?
MAYBE HE THOUGHT WE WERE MOJO! I GET US CONFUSED ALL THE TIME!
THAT WAS NO MISTAKE!
I PURPOSEFULLY BLASTED YOUR SILLY LITTLE HEROES, TOWNSVILLE! THAT'S THE NAME OF THIS PLACE, RIGHT?
I THINK SO!
REALLY, NOBODY SHOULD VOTE FOR THIS GUY.
FOR I AM GAL-CACTUS, SPACE CACTUS!
CUTE RHYME!
...EATER OF TOWNS!
OH.
...AND I'M HUNGRY! PREPARE TO BE EATEN, TOWNSVILLE!
WELL, THIS WAS A TWIST.
TELL ME ABOUT IT.
DITTO.

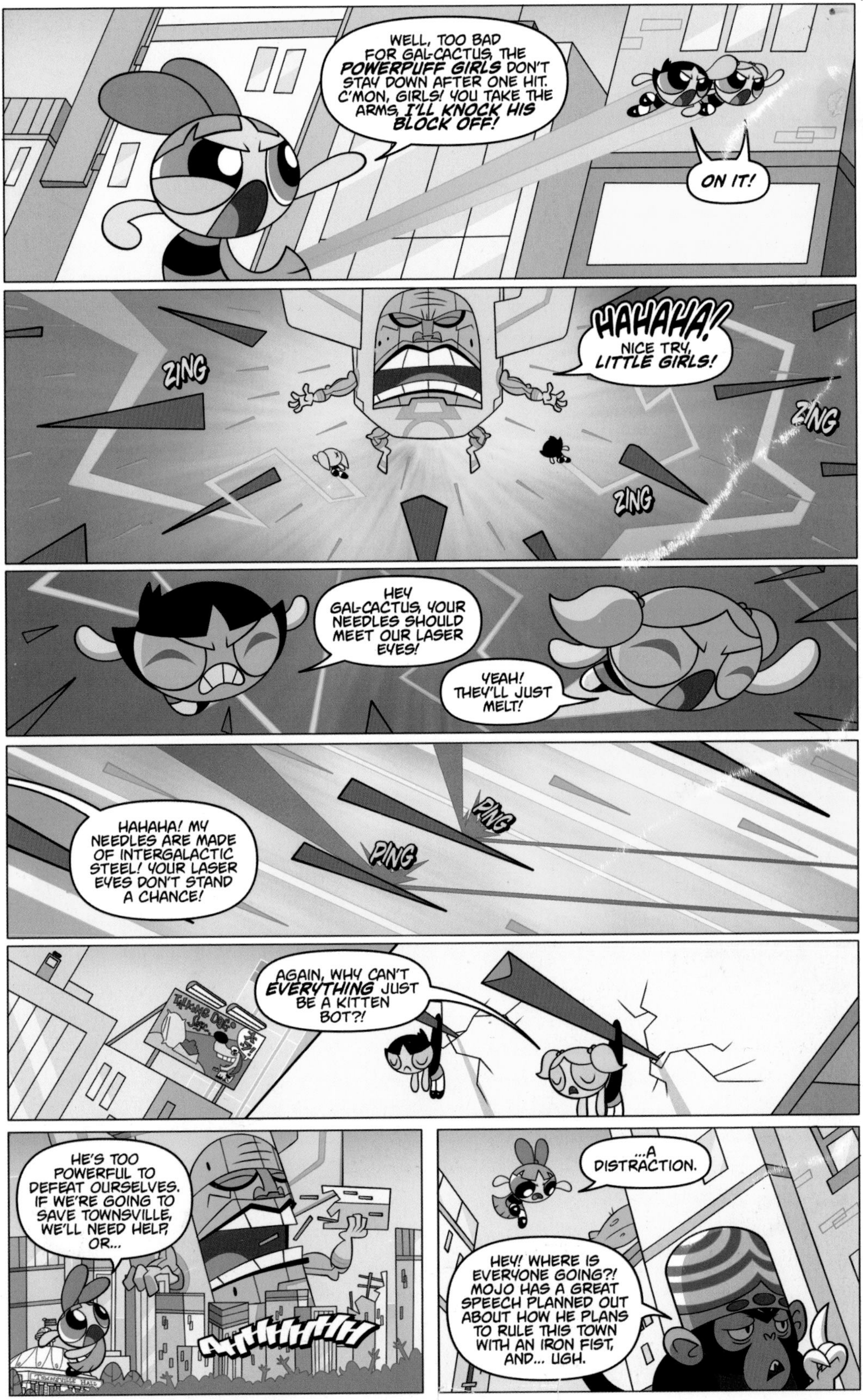
WELL, TOO BAD FOR GAL-CACTUS, THE POWERPUFF GIRLS DON'T STAY DOWN AFTER ONE HIT. C'MON, GIRLS! YOU TAKE THE ARMS, I'LL KNOCK HIS BLOCK OFF!
ON IT!
HAHAHA! NICE TRY, LITTLE GIRLS!
ZING
ZING
ZING
HEY GAL-CACTUS, YOUR NEEDLES SHOULD MEET OUR LASER EYES!
YEAH! THEY'LL JUST MELT!
HAHAHA! MY NEEDLES ARE MADE OF INTERGALACTIC STEEL! YOUR LASER EYES DON'T STAND A CHANCE!
PING
PING
AGAIN, WHY CAN'T EVERYTHING JUST BE A KITTEN BOT?!
HE'S TOO POWERFUL TO DEFEAT OURSELVES. IF WE'RE GOING TO SAVE TOWNSVILLE, WE'LL NEED HELP, OR...
AHHHHHH
...A DISTRACTION.
HEY! WHERE IS EVERYONE GOING?! MOJO HAS A GREAT SPEECH PLANNED OUT ABOUT HOW HE PLANS TO RULE THIS TOWN WITH AN IRON FIST, AND... UGH.

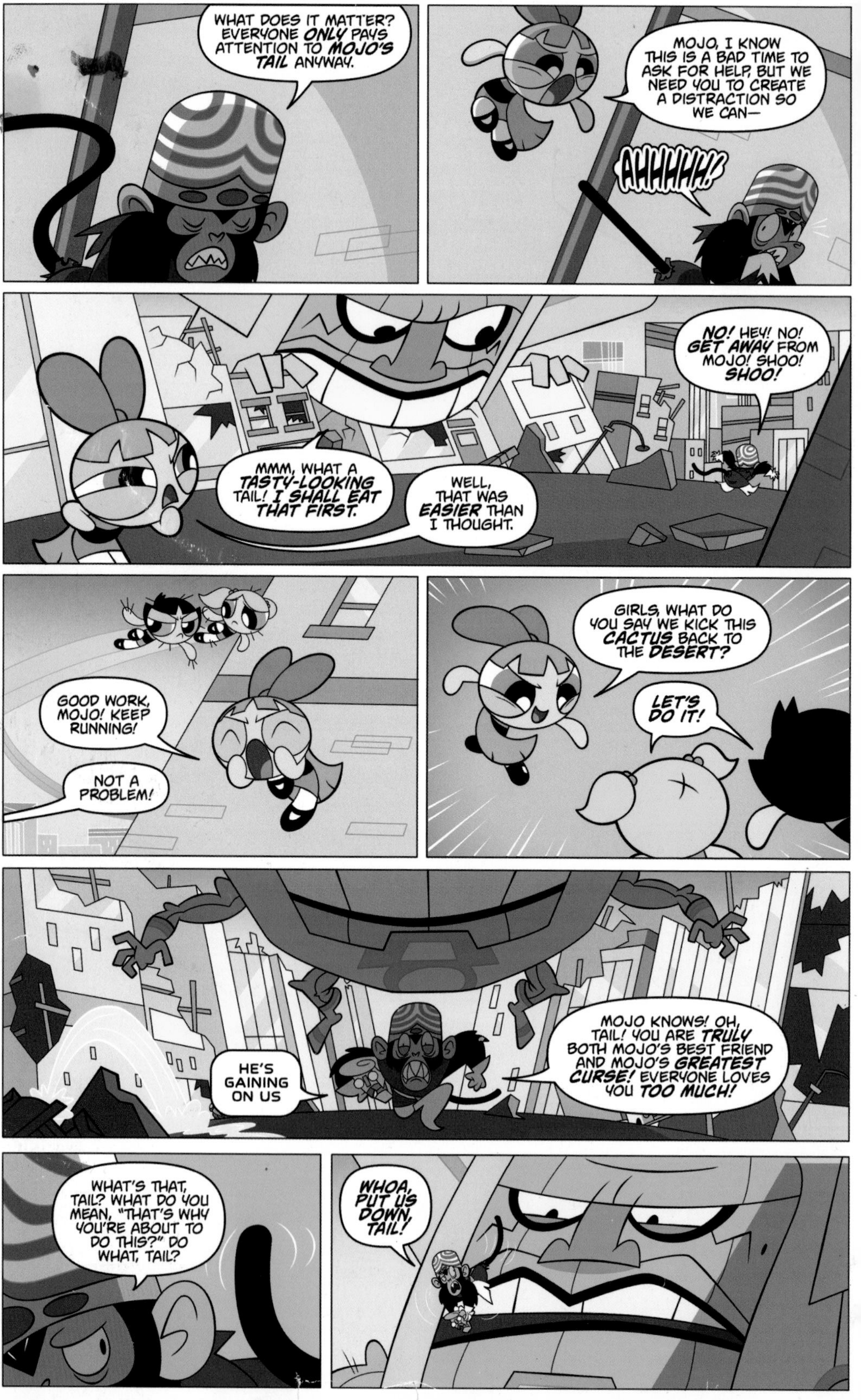

WHAT DOES IT MATTER? EVERYONE ONLY PAYS ATTENTION TO MOJO'S TAIL ANYWAY.
MOJO, I KNOW THIS IS A BAD TIME TO ASK FOR HELP, BUT WE NEED YOU TO CREATE A DISTRACTION SO WE CAN—
AHHHHH!
NO! HEY! NO! GET AWAY FROM MOJO! SHOO! SHOO!
MMM, WHAT A TASTY-LOOKING TAIL! I SHALL EAT THAT FIRST.
WELL, THAT WAS EASIER THAN I THOUGHT.
GOOD WORK, MOJO! KEEP RUNNING!
NOT A PROBLEM!
GIRLS, WHAT DO YOU SAY WE KICK THIS CACTUS BACK TO THE DESERT?
LET'S DO IT!
HE'S GAINING ON US
MOJO KNOWS! OH, TAIL! YOU ARE TRULY BOTH MOJO'S BEST FRIEND AND MOJO'S GREATEST CURSE! EVERYONE LOVES YOU TOO MUCH!
WHAT'S THAT, TAIL? WHAT DO YOU MEAN, "THAT'S WHY YOU'RE ABOUT TO DO THIS?" DO WHAT, TAIL?
WHOA, PUT US DOWN, TAIL!

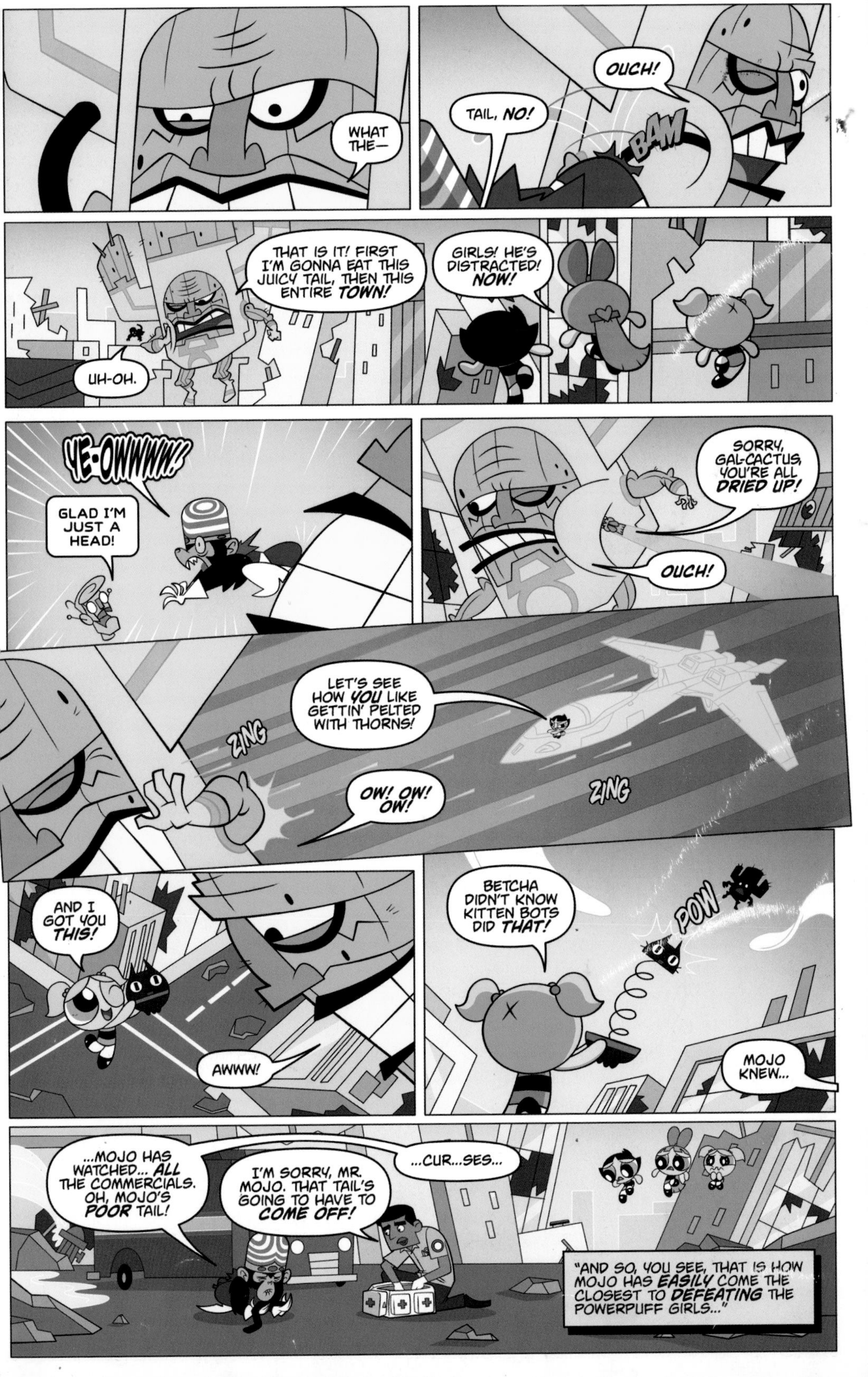
WHAT THE—
OUCH!
TAIL, NO!
BAM
THAT IS IT! FIRST I'M GONNA EAT THIS JUICY TAIL, THEN THIS ENTIRE TOWN!
UH-OH.
GIRLS! HE'S DISTRACTED! NOW!
YE-OWWWW!
GLAD I'M JUST A HEAD!
SORRY, GAL-CACTUS, YOU'RE ALL DRIED UP!
OUCH!
LET'S SEE HOW YOU LIKE GETTIN' PELTED WITH THORNS!
ZING
ZING
OW! OW! OW!
AND I GOT YOU THIS!
AWWW!
BETCHA DIDN'T KNOW KITTEN BOTS DID THAT!
POW
MOJO KNEW...
...MOJO HAS WATCHED... ALL THE COMMERCIALS. OH, MOJO'S POOR TAIL!
...CUR...SES...
I'M SORRY, MR. MOJO. THAT TAIL'S GOING TO HAVE TO COME OFF!
"AND SO, YOU SEE, THAT IS HOW MOJO HAS EASILY COME THE CLOSEST TO DEFEATING THE POWERPUFF GIRLS..."

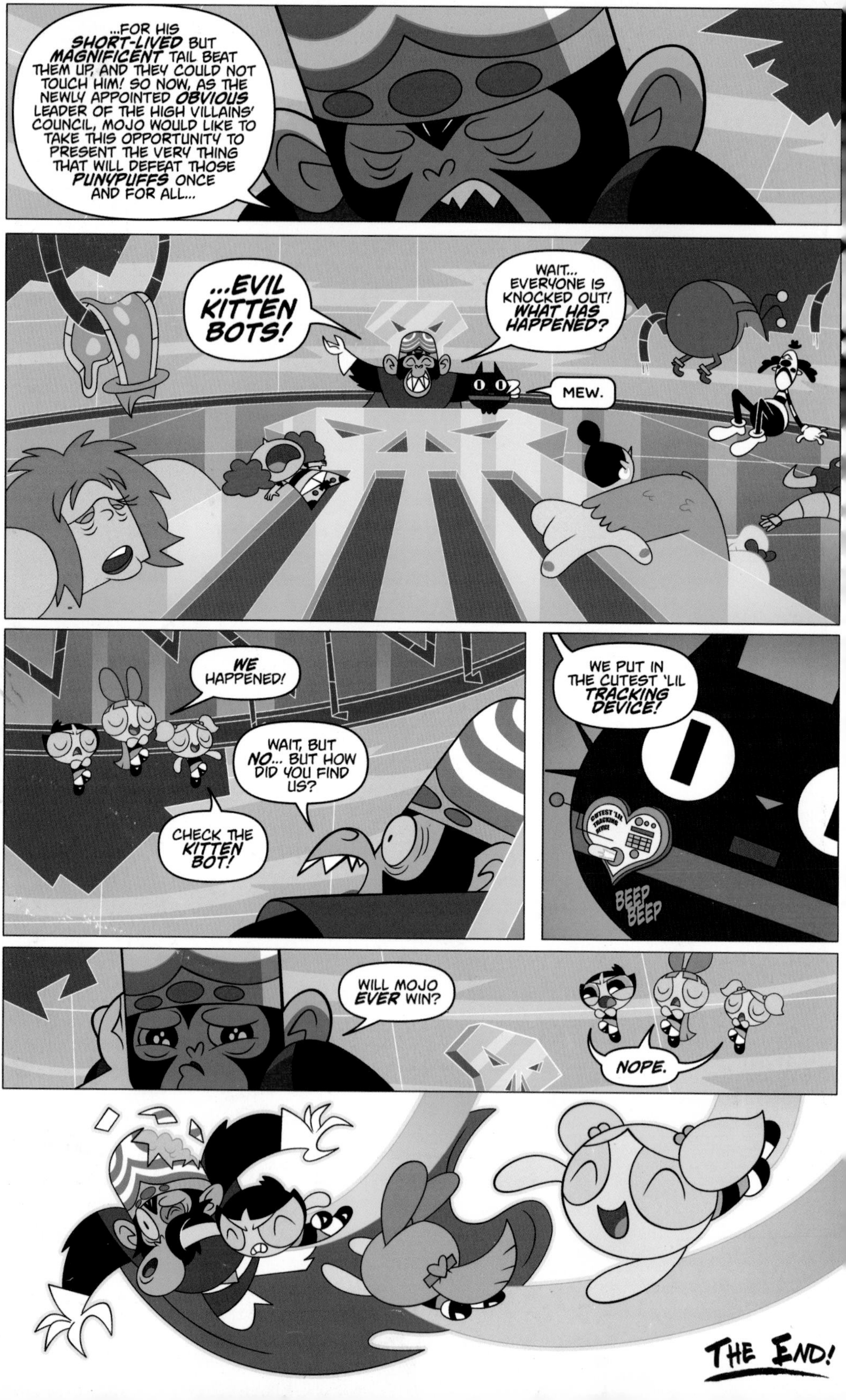

...FOR HIS SHORT-LIVED BUT MAGNIFICENT TAIL BEAT THEM UP, AND THEY COULD NOT TOUCH HIM! SO NOW, AS THE NEWLY APPOINTED OBVIOUS LEADER OF THE HIGH VILLAINS' COUNCIL, MOJO WOULD LIKE TO TAKE THIS OPPORTUNITY TO PRESENT THE VERY THING THAT WILL DEFEAT THOSE PUNYPUFFS ONCE AND FOR ALL...
...EVIL KITTEN BOTS!
WAIT... EVERYONE IS KNOCKED OUT! WHAT HAS HAPPENED?
MEW.
WE HAPPENED!
WAIT, BUT NO... BUT HOW DID YOU FIND US?
CHECK THE KITTEN BOT!
WE PUT IN THE CUTEST 'LIL TRACKING DEVICE!
CUTEST 'LIL TRACKING DEVICE
BEEP BEEP
WILL MOJO EVER WIN?
NOPE.
THE END!

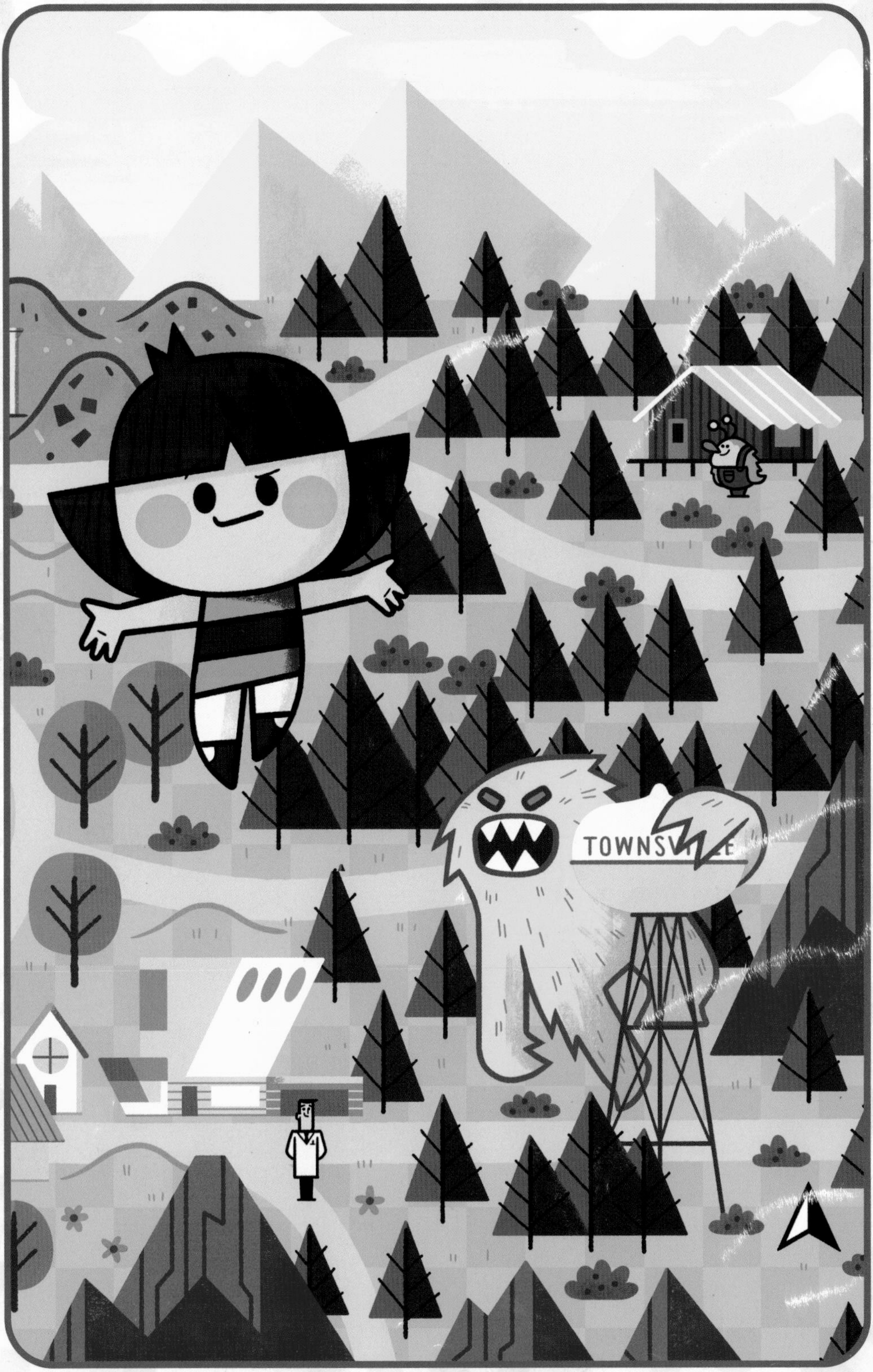
TOWNSV

Cover Art by **Andrew Kolb**

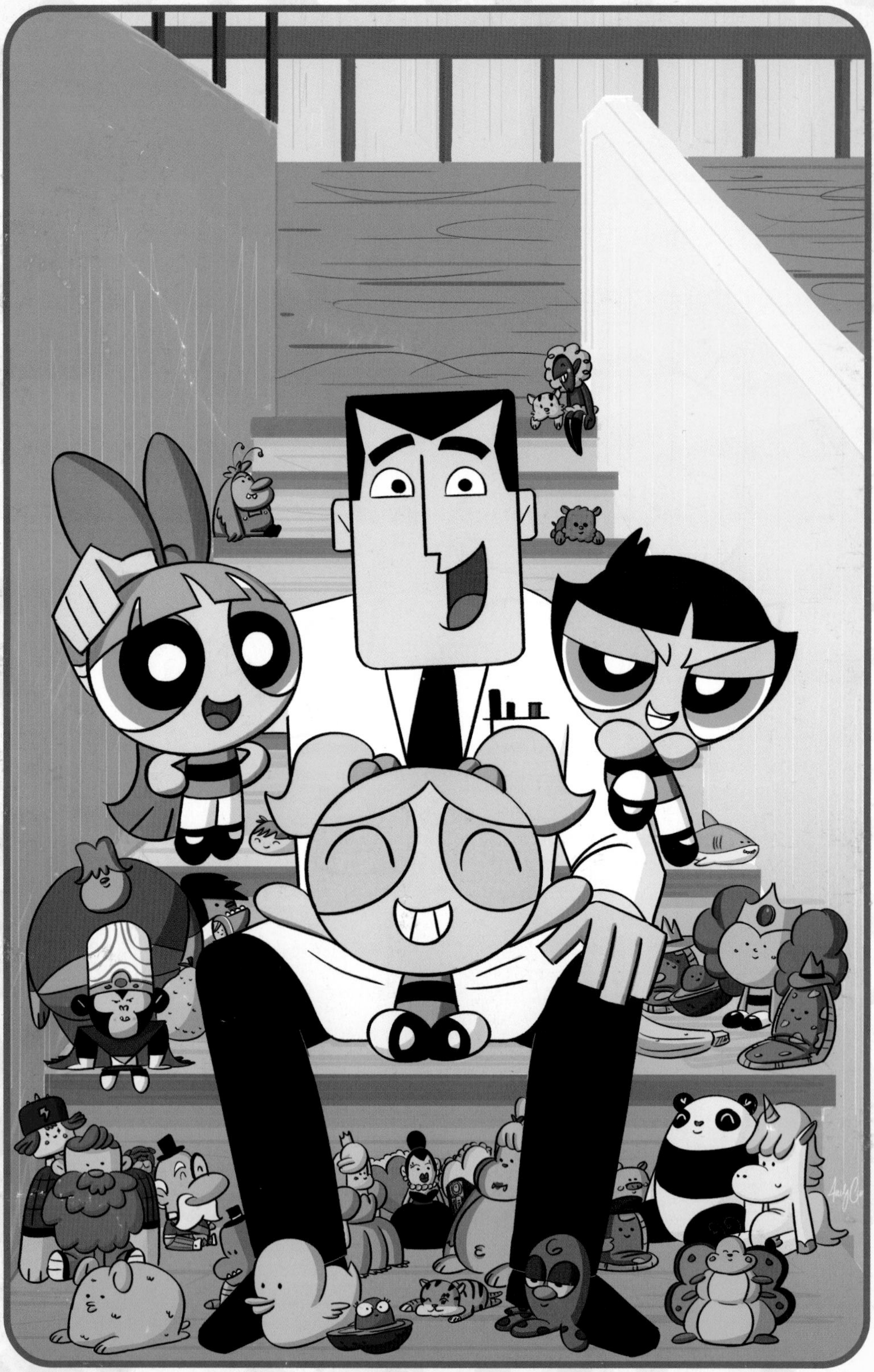

Cover Art by **Andy Cung**

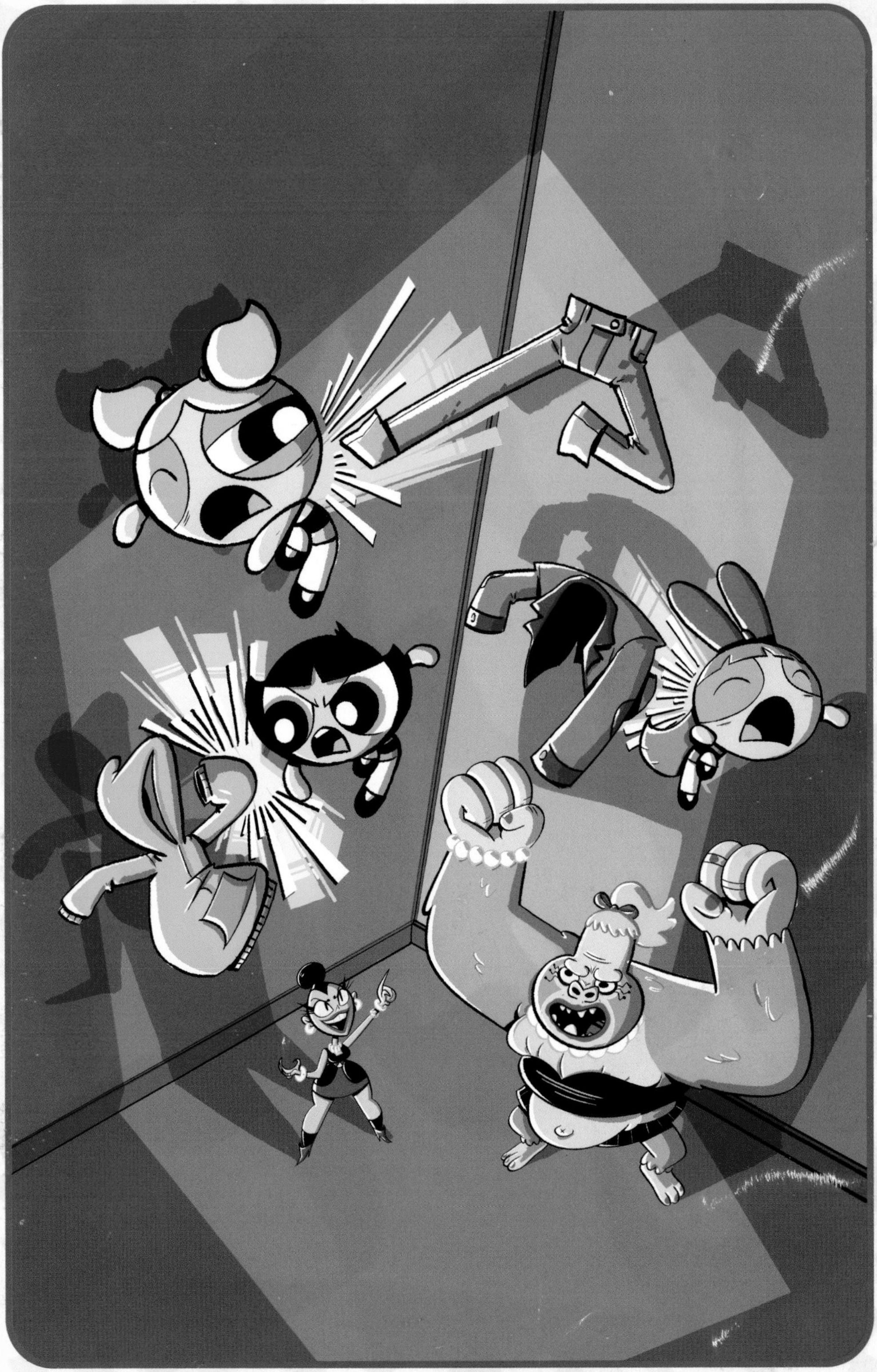

Cover Art by **Benjamin Carow**

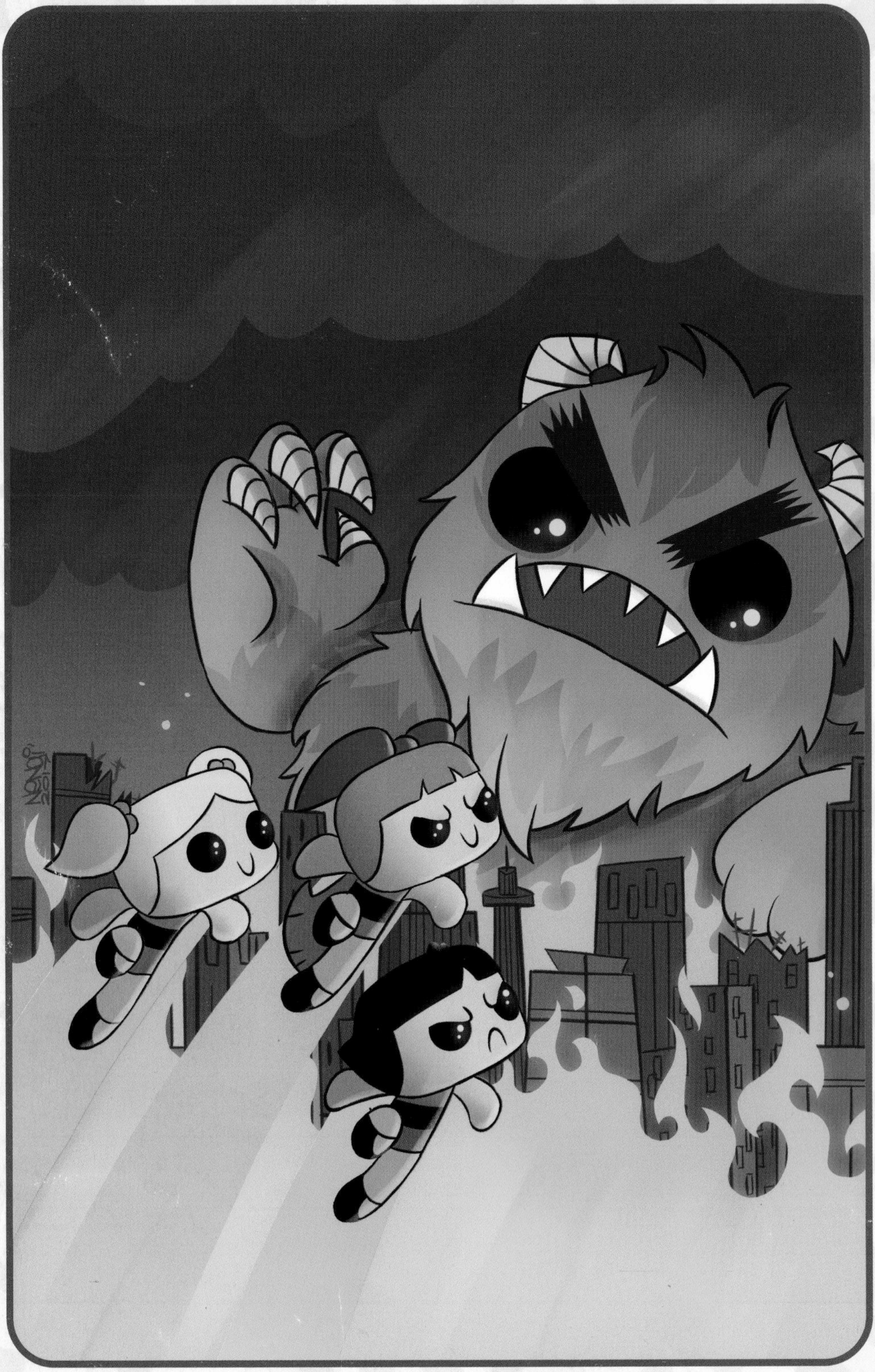

Cover Art by **Nnenna Ijiomah**